a bit of murder between friends

KNITTING, TEA, GOSSIP ... VENGEANCE

VIGILAUNTIE JUSTICE #1

ELLIOTT HAY

Protect Trans kids!

eh.

White Hart Fiction
·INCLUSIVE STORIES·

A Bit of Murder Between Friends (Vigilauntie Justice #1)

Knitting, tea, gossip ... vengeance

Print edition ISBN: 978-1-7397681-3-3

www.whitehartfiction.co.uk

Most recent update: 3 July 2023

Editing by:

•Michelle Meade of Michelle Meade Reads

•Hannah McCall of Black Cat Editorial Services

Cover art by: Ilknur Mustu

❀ Created with Vellum

content warnings

This work contains the following:

- While none takes place on-page, there are discussions of sexual assault throughout
- Mentions of transphobia
- Accidental cannibalism

The *Vigilauntie Justice* books are cosy(ish) noir(ish) stories set in London. They do have on-page violence, including murder, but it's never graphic. There's minimal swearing and no romance or sex – but there's heaps of queer content and found family.

author's note

This book is written in British English. If you're used to reading American English, some of the spelling and punctuation may seem unusual. I promise, it's totally safe.

This story also features a number of Canadianisms. Sadly, I cannot promise these are safe. You may find yourself involuntarily wearing a touque and craving Timbits and a double-double. It can't be helped. Seek treatment immediately.

CHAPTER 1

in which our heroine sets out on a quest

As Baz steered her mobility scooter into the intersection, the screech of a horn almost gave her a heart attack. The driver turning left was trying to cut in front of her.

Heat flushed her cheeks. She opened her mouth to apologise but before she could say anything, a person walking in the opposite direction bellowed at the driver. 'You've got a red, mate!'

Sure enough, when Baz looked up, she found that pedestrians and vehicles heading straight on had the right of way. Drivers turning left still faced a red. 'What a confusing intersection.' She wasn't sure whether she was speaking to herself or to the angry driver. To the Good Samaritan she added, 'Thank you.'

The pedestrian nodded and carried on walking. Baz squeezed the scooter's accelerator with the fingers of her right hand.

Before long, she was wending her way along Deptford Broadway, heading west. If she followed this route for another six kilometres, she'd end up somewhere in the vicinity of

London Bridge. It still amazed her how close to the heart of London she was.

But she wasn't going nearly that far today – just a short jaunt.

In the last few months, Baz had accepted a sizeable financial settlement, signed divorce papers, sold half of her former house to her now ex-husband, left her job, said goodbye to all her friends, moved her entire life thousands of kilometres away, and bought a new flat.

Oh, and she'd come out of the proverbial closet to live as the woman she'd finally accepted herself as.

To say she felt a bit lost and alone in the whirlwind would be something of an understatement. Would her old self have immediately apologised to that driver without knowing who was in the wrong? She wasn't sure.

Five minutes later, Baz parked her scooter on the little strip of pavement next to Wellbeloved Café's outside seating area. It was a beautiful September day, the sun shining brightly over south-east London. The pain bit into her knee when she stood up and she tried to hide her grimace. She smiled at a young man walking past and gave a cheerful wave to his toddler.

'W.H. Wellbeloved: Butchers & Graziers' proclaimed the sign on the pebble-dashed south wall. Baz found herself wondering how long it had been since a butcher had actually occupied the building. She walked the few steps to the door but paused outside and took a deep breath.

'Come on, Baz. You can do this.' She pursed her lips, ever-so-slightly smearing her rose-coloured lipstick. 'They're not monsters.' She cast her eyes to the window to her right. 'Look at them.' Why did making friends have to be so hard? Children did it all the time – why couldn't adults? And, more specifically, why couldn't she?

Adjusting her shoulder bag and smoothing down the fabric

of her lavender cotton dress, she took one last deep breath and pushed open the door of the small coffee shop. Ever since she'd started hormone therapy a few months back, her senses had become stronger, more vibrant. The scents of the shop filled her with warmth and comfort. Freshly roasted coffee was the dominant aroma, but it mingled with cinnamon and sugar and fresh-baked pastry.

The young woman behind the counter – Olena was her name – looked up and smiled. 'Morning.' She held a hand out for the expected takeaway cup. 'The usual?'

Baz had been visiting Wellbeloved every day for the past two weeks and the staff – two women – had already learnt her order. They worked hard to make her feel so comfortable and accepted. She held out her empty hands, palms up. 'Yes, please. Though I think I'll stay in this time.' She could do this, she reassured herself.

Olena nodded and rang up the order. 'Go ahead and take a seat.'

Waist-height and below, the walls were painted a very fashionable green. Higher up, shelves were lined with pieces of art. There were small, framed paintings and photographs, knitted goods, pottery. All sorts of lovely things. Overall, the effect was vibrant but tasteful. The creativity on display brought a smile to Baz's face.

She took a deep breath. Putting a hand to the solid stone wall, she ducked through the door into the shop's second room – originally a separate building, she suspected. The place must have been several hundred years old; the walls were thick and the door between the rooms wasn't quite high enough for modern adults. At five foot seven, Baz wasn't exactly short – but she was hardly tall. She could probably walk through without smacking her head on the lintel – just. Better to be safe than sorry.

You can do this, she reminded herself. Not aloud, of course. She didn't want anyone to think she was a bit batty. It was enough that some people assumed that just from looking at her.

People could be so judgemental.

But her loneliness pushed her to overcome her fears. Pulling her shoulders back, Baz approached the three women sitting nearest the window. 'Good morning, ladies. My name is Barbara, um, Baz. I'm new to Deptford and I wondered if I might join you?'

Just then, what Baz had taken for a heavy carpet lifted up off the floor. And up ... and up ... and up. After a few moments, she found herself face to face – well, more like crotch to face – with the biggest, most beautiful Alsatian she'd ever seen.

He wagged his tail and licked her hand. Smiling, she scratched his head. He reminded her of her own dog. Well, her ex's dog. For a while, after they'd split up, he'd brought the dog to Baz's on weekends.

Gosh, she missed that dog. If she wasn't careful, she'd burst into tears. And then what would these women think of her?

A full-figured Black woman with a knitting project resting on an ample bosom looked up at her. 'In my day,' she said in a local accent, 'men were men and women were women and—'

Baz felt heat rise in her cheeks. She knew that – to most people – she looked like a man in a dress. As much as she knew to the very core of her being that she was a woman, she sometimes feared the world would never see her that way.

'In your day, Madge,' said an elderly white woman with spiky hot pink hair and an equally spiky choker necklace, 'nurses weren't allowed to have sex. Never stopped you.' With an encouraging wink, she grinned at Baz. Her tartan jacket was covered in pins and badges. Baz couldn't read them from even the short distance between them – though she was sure she spied a rainbow flag.

The pink-haired punk woman addressed Baz. 'Pay Madge no heed. I promise she's not actually transphobic – she just likes to stick her sanctimonious nose into people's business for no reason at all.'

'Sanctimony doesn't come into it.' Knitting needles still clicking away, Madge studied Baz. 'What I meant was I would like to understand – are you a woman or are you not?' She waved a hand, still clutching her knitting, in Baz's direction. 'I'm not asking what's in your pants – just how I should think of you. I've never met a transgender person before and I'm not up on all the newfangled terminology. If that seems rude, I apologise.'

Baz's stomach twisted inside her. She wanted to flee. Or to argue back. But her fight-or-flight instinct was firmly stuck on *freeze*. Alas, the arrival of a young woman served only to further cement Baz's inability to move.

CHAPTER 2

in which we are left to wonder how it's possible to have 3.5 husbands

THE NEW ARRIVAL brandished a stack of brightly coloured papers. 'Hi. The woman at the front counter said the manager isn't here today? And that I should talk to you lot? I'm Jenna? I'm from Goldsmiths? You know, the uni up the road?'

All of her sentences seemed to end in question marks for reasons that weren't clear to Baz.

Baz was desperately looking for an excuse to make an exit but the giant brute of a dog sat down on her feet, his fur tickling her bare toes through her orthopaedic sandals.

The third woman at the table – a white-haired woman with red lipstick and a cheerful face – carried on knitting as if she were completely unaware of everything going on around her.

The punk woman glanced over at Baz and rolled her eyes. 'Goodness me. And here I've lived in this area for decades without ever noticing we had a university. What is the point you are trying to make?' A hint of a grin pulled at the corners of her mouth.

'Oh, er, hi. Sorry? Right. Well, I wanted to know if I could put up a poster?' The young woman clutched the papers with one hand and adjusted her hat – some sort of old-fashioned train conductor's hat – with the other.

Madge sucked her teeth. 'What are you selling?'

'Oh, no. Nothing like that.' Jenna danced from foot to foot. The dog prodded at Baz's hand with his nose, so she obliged him by stroking his massive head. 'It's about a series of sexual assaults in the neighbourhood? I don't know if you've heard about what's been happening?'

That caught Baz's attention and she leant forwards to get a closer look at the papers in Jenna's hands.

The movement, slight at it was, caught Jenna's attention. She startled then blanched as she faced Baz. 'Why are you skulking there? You think we can't tell what you are?'

Just when Baz was praying that the earth would open up and swallow her whole, Madge leapt to her feet – no mean feat for a woman of her advanced years and considerable girth. She brought her hand, still clutching a knitting needle, to Jenna's face. 'How dare you, young lady. This is my good friend, Beverley—'

'Barbara,' the pink-haired woman corrected.

Madge nodded and continued without missing a beat. 'As I said, Barbara. Did no one teach you manners, young lady? You will address your elders with respect. You will call her Auntie or...' She leant around Jenna and faced Baz. 'Sorry, dear. What's your surname?'

Somehow Baz found the strength to reply, still unsure quite what was happening. 'Spencer.'

Madge turned back to the student. 'Or as Mrs Spencer.'

Heat rose in Baz's face but she felt obliged to correct Madge. 'It's *Ms* Spencer, actually.'

The pink-haired woman nodded approvingly.

'Ms Spencer,' Madge continued. 'Now, young lady, if you'd like to tell us what your business is, you will treat us with dignity and respect. You will not come into *our* establishment and behave with insolence. And, Barbara, dear, with your knee in the state it's in, you should sit down before Cookie presses you into the wall.'

'Wha— How did—'

Madge shook her head. 'Not now, dear. Just take your seat and let's hear what young Jenna has to say about these assaults.'

Baz did as she was bid and Madge returned to her own chair. Cookie crouched down and settled back into what was clearly his customary place under the small table between the ladies.

Once she was seated, Baz looked up. Jenna's face flushed. The young woman furrowed her brow as she opened and closed her mouth. 'Sorry. I didn't mean...' The tops of her ears were almost burgundy as she crossed her arms in front of herself. She took a step backwards as she looked Baz straight in the eye. 'I meant you're a cop.'

Jenna looked from one to the other of the rest of the group. 'You can tell she's a cop, right? It's plain as day! Look at the way she stands – how she holds herself, her eyes taking in everything going on in here. She looks like she's memorising every last detail. And she's probably wearing a wire!'

Madge and the pink-haired woman glanced at the silent woman across the table. But she continued knitting. She'd still shown no sign of being aware there was anything going on.

'Retired,' said Baz. It didn't seem like the time to mention that she'd actually been a civilian investigator working alongside the police. Most people didn't understand the difference anyways. And she'd absorbed enough of the body language and mannerisms that people often presumed she was a cop as soon as they met her.

'Oh, my gosh.' Jenna slapped her hands to her face. 'You didn't think I meant about you being, you know, trans, did you?

Because that's totally not it. That's not even a thing. Honestly, one of my friends is trans.'

The pink-haired woman – Baz told herself she really should find out her name – leant forwards in her chair, pressing her thin chest against the screen of her laptop. 'Young woman. We are very old. If you don't get to the point soon, we'll likely all be dead before you finish telling us why you are interrupting our conversation.'

Jenna startled – something she did quite often from Baz's limited experience of her. 'Right. Sorry. Er... There's a sexual predator in New Cross and Deptford. He's preying on women as they get off buses, you know? He follows them and then attacks in public? There've been six incidents that we're aware of over the past four months. Only the police aren't doing anything?' She looked at Baz, sneering. 'They're not even warning women about the danger.'

'Well, it's the Met,' said the hitherto silent woman. 'What do you expect? Filth.'

Jenna's eyes opened wide as saucers and she nodded solemnly. 'Exactly. Since when does the Met give a toss what happens to working-class women?' Though, truth be told, judging by the sound of her accent, Baz suspected Jenna didn't know the first thing about the lives of working-class people. 'Just ask that woman who was murdered by a Met officer a few years ago, you know?'

'Or look up the rates of domestic violence amongst serving officers,' said the pink-haired woman. Baz cursed herself for not knowing her name yet.

Jenna nodded so hard, Baz feared she might injure herself. 'Exactly.' She shook her head as if to clear it. 'Anyhow, as I was saying, the Filth' – Jenna cast a sideways glance at Baz – 'aren't doing anything. So me and some of my fellow students are organising a sort of grassroots campaign to raise awareness? To encourage women and girls to exercise caution, especially when getting off the bus? Sometimes women have to take matters into our own hands – you know what I mean?'

Madge and her friends exchanged glances. 'We are in agreement on that point, I believe. You may post one of your papers on the noticeboard by the front door.'

Baz cleared her throat. 'My granddaughter used to teach self-defence classes at her school. She's just started at Goldsmiths. Perhaps you could talk to her. Maybe set up something similar here?'

Jenna eyed Baz suspiciously for a moment. 'That's actually not a terrible idea.'

Baz reached a hand out. 'Are there contact details on your leaflets? If you leave me one, I'll get Daisy to contact you.'

Jenna's eyes opened wide once again. 'Daisy? You mean Daisy Spencer? She's in some of my classes?'

A warmth spread through Baz's chest. 'You know my granddaughter?'

Just then, Olena appeared, bearing a tray. She set a small teapot and mug in front of Baz. 'There you go, my love. Sorry for the wait. There's some oat milk for you as well.' She added a small jug.

'Thank you, dear.' Baz was beginning to see what she'd been missing out on by taking her tea as takeaway for the past two weeks. Even if she didn't end up becoming friends with this trio, this place was still a delightful find.

Jenna stroked her long, brown hair and glanced towards the exit. 'So, er, I'll just go ahead and put one of these up by the door, shall I?'

The pink-haired woman was busy typing away on her computer. 'You do that.'

Baz wondered what she was writing. Based on what she

knew of the woman so far, she figured it must be something intellectual. Maybe she was an academic.

Madge returned her attention to her knitting. She nodded once without looking up.

Baz, who'd been about to pour herself a cup of tea, set the pot down and raised a hand. 'And don't forget to talk to Daisy about those self-defence classes.'

Jenna, who was already in the metre-thick doorway to the café's main room, turned back to face Baz. 'I will. That's a really good idea. Thank you.' She twisted her lips a bit. 'And I'm sorry about before. You know with the ... sorry.' She headed through the doorway and disappeared. A few moments later, she reappeared on the other side of the window, unlocked a bike, and rode off. Baz shook her head at the thought of her riding without a helmet.

The pink-haired woman peered at her over the top of her laptop. 'Well then. We should get on with the introductions and then we'll discuss what we're going to do about this miscreant who's preying upon our community.'

Both Madge and the silent woman nodded.

Baz felt naked without some sort of craft or project to work on. *They must think me so lazy.* She really ought to undertake ... something. She considered knitting but she didn't want the others to think she was copying them. Perhaps embroidery? Her grandmother had taught her when she was a child but she'd not tried her hand at it for decades.

The pink-haired woman picked up her mug and leant back in her chair. 'I'm Peggy Trent. You've already met my young ward here, Cookie.' She prodded the great beast of a dog with a Doc Martens clad foot.

Baz smiled, delighted to finally have a name for the intriguing woman. 'Pleasure to make your acquaintance, Peggy.'

Peggy dipped her head towards Madge, the full-figured

Black woman on her right, who said, 'I'm Mrs Margaret Dixon. You may call me Madge.'

'Lovely to meet you.'

With her left hand – short fingernails painted black, Baz noted – Peggy touched the knee of the third woman. 'Carole, sweetheart, you should introduce yourself.'

Carole looked up, making a face as if she'd only just noticed Baz. 'Oh, hello. I'm Carole Ballard. My family rose to prominence in this neighbourhood. We started off as little more than a backstreet gang but, over the years, we built up quite an empire. A *criminal* empire, with arms all throughout the British Isles.'

Baz frowned, unsure what to say.

Peggy appeared to fight a smile. 'Carole, love, that's the plot of *Peaky Blinders*. You know – from the telly?'

Carole nodded solemnly. 'Well, they had to get their ideas from somewhere, didn't they?' She carried on knitting.

So it was like that then, was it? Baz breathed the steam from her cup of tea. She smiled as she took a sip. Perfection.

Peggy waved her hand in the other woman's direction. 'My Carole has quite the imagination. Half her stories are complete codswallop.'

Madge raised both eyebrows. 'Or all her stories are half cockamamie.'

Carole's knitting needles clacked as she continued working on her scarf or blanket or whatever it was. 'No one's ever sure which half,' she said with perfect seriousness. 'But my Harvey loved me more than life itself. No matter how many exotic dancers, art dealers, and Mercedes salespeople he slept with.' Baz shook her head, unsure of what she was supposed to do with this information.

'Did you know,' Carole continued, 'Madge here has been married three and a half times? And Peggy says marriage is an inherently patriarchal institution designed to perpetuate gender inequality.'

Peggy gave a firm nod but Baz's mind was awhirl. She turned to Madge. 'Three and a *half* times?'

Madge studied what she was knitting and undid a few stitches. 'That's right.' She didn't offer any further details and Baz got the sense it would be rude to pry.

'Madge and I have been friends for five years and we were neighbours for several years before that.' Peggy set her empty mug down on the table. 'I still have no idea what that means.'

Madge yawned. 'Peggy fancies she was part of the Bromley Contingent – though in truth she only met them a few times at shows.'

'It was more than a few times.' Peggy looked indignant. 'And, actually, I've always been into all sorts of bands, not just the Sex Pistols.'

Madge chuckled. 'But Peggy had a decade on the rest of that crowd – and she had a full-time job. She couldn't be touring all over the continent, chasing after her fancy boys.'

Baz could actually hear Peggy's teeth grinding. 'It was never about *boys*!'

Baz wondered why Peggy's response was so strong but before she could think about it Madge's sharp gaze was on her. 'Now your turn, dear. I assume this knee of yours has something to do with why a youngster such as yourself would be retired.'

At sixty-two, Baz was flattered and, truth be told, a bit amused to be referred to as a youngster. But more curious. 'How did you notice? My knee, I mean. And, yes, that's exactly why I was medicalled out.'

Peggy, who was sneaking glances at her laptop during the conversation, looked up. 'Not the Met, I take it.'

'No, ma'am.' Baz shook her head. 'Edmonton.'

Peggy arched a painted eyebrow. 'You don't sound like you're from north London. And that's still the Met's jurisdiction anyhow.'

'What?'

'She means the one in Canada,' said Carole, pausing her knitting. Or was that crocheting? Baz always struggled to tell the difference. 'Didn't that pig farmer live in Edmonton for a while?'

Baz blinked, feeling somewhat flummoxed by Carole. 'Edmonton, yes. Carole's right. It's in Alberta. Um, I was with the RCMP.' She took a sip of her tea, which was barely above room temperature by this point. 'I was born right here in Lewisham. My family lived in Deptford when I was a b— When I was a child. We moved to Canada when I was twelve. And to answer your question, Madge, yes, it was my knee. Fractured my patella and tore my meniscus on the job.' There was no need to tell them she'd been hit by an ambulance.

Taking a deep breath, Baz ran a hand over her shoulder-length ginger wig. She'd started growing her own hair out a few months before, but it was only just past her ears these days. 'How did you, um, how'd you notice?'

Peggy waved a hand in Madge's direction. 'Madge was an orthopaedic nurse. One of the first nurse practitioners in the UK.'

'You favour your right leg when you walk.' Madge's lips twitched. 'There's a certain stiffness in the way you walk. I figured you'd had an arthroscopic partial meniscectomy. Maybe even a full meniscectomy. Judging by how you move, I'd guess you're no more than four months out from the surgery. Maybe six if it was full.'

Baz was impressed. 'It's been six months. And yes, it was a full meniscithingy.' She spent a moment watching the people

outside the café's window. 'Now about these sexual assaults...
Were you ladies aware?'

Peggy and Madge exchanged glances. Baz couldn't tell what
the looks meant ... but she was one hundred per cent certain
they meant something. She felt confident whole conversations
had been conveyed in that moment.

Madge did that thing again, sucking air in through her
teeth. Peggy cocked her head to one side and said, 'Well.'

But it was Carole who crossed her arms over her chest and
declared, 'It's no good, is it?'

It turned out the ladies did know about the attacks. And
Carole had nothing good to say about the perpetrator – or the
police. And what she did say ... well, it wasn't fit for repeating
in polite society. Carole had quite the mouth on her.

'In my day, we didn't tolerate this sort of thing. A couple of
my lads would pop round and have a quiet word and then the
community would all come together to clean up the mess, so
there was nothing left for the Filth to find.'

Baz wondered if she should feel unnerved by all that but
both Peggy and Madge simply nodded while carrying on with
their typing and knitting, respectively.

CHAPTER 3

wherein we learn of carole's unusual hobby

THE NEXT MORNING, Peggy and Carole held hands as they walked across the car park that separated the home they shared from the café. Cookie walked calmly alongside Peggy. The group met up with Madge just before they arrived.

When Madge pushed open the front door, Baz was already at the counter. She was accompanied by a tall young woman with blond hair and exquisite bone structure. The young woman's frilly high-necked blouse was paired with a tie that put Peggy in mind of that chicken man. Colonel Sanders. Her backpack was covered with a host of pins and badges, one of which was emblazoned with a pink and blue dinosaur and the words 'trans rights or I bites'.

Despite herself, Peggy warmed to the young woman.

Baz tapped her phone on the machine to pay for the order then turned back to face her new friends. 'Ladies, good morning. I'd like you to meet my granddaughter, Daisy. Daisy, these charming women are — from left to right — Madge, Peggy, and Carole.'

Uh oh. Madge didn't approve of young people referring to

their elders by their first names. Peggy was amused by Madge's discomfort.

'Lovely to meet you all. Nan's told me a bit about you. I'm so pleased she's made some friends.' Daisy seemed very sweet.

Peggy hated sweet; give her salty any day.

Madge raised a floral-print clad arm and gestured towards the woman behind the counter – a different woman from the day before. 'And I see you've met our business partner in this establishment. This is my youngest, Sarah. Sarah, you know my friend Ms Spencer, don't you?'

When the old butcher had retired in 2021, Sarah had approached her mum with an idea to convert the space to a coffee shop. Madge had taken the proposal to Peggy and Carole. Sarah gained three investors – silent business partners. Well, silent in theory if not always in practice. And somehow Sarah had found herself convinced that what she had really wanted all along was a café cum arts and crafts gallery.

That was one of Madge's gifts. Not only could she bring people round to see her point of view, but somehow they were always left with the impression that they'd thought of it first.

Madge and Carole's handiwork adorned the shop's walls and shelves. Peggy's work was sold elsewhere.

Sarah wiped her hands on her apron and nodded at each of the newcomers in turn. 'Ms Spencer. Daisy. It's always nice to put names to faces.'

'Please, call me Baz.'

After greeting Sarah, Daisy squatted and held out a dainty hand – every nail a different colour – to Cookie. 'And you must be Cookie. Aren't you the most handsome boy?' The dog gave her hand a good sniff and allowed himself to be fussed over. Daisy looked up at Baz. 'You were right – he really does look like Sophie. Bigger, though.'

Sarah smiled at the group. 'Go ahead and take your seats, ladies. I'll bring everything over to you in a few minutes.'

Baz offered her thanks before she and Daisy followed the others into the café's second room.

Daisy looked up at Peggy. 'If you ever need anyone to walk him, I'd be happy to take him out for a bit.'

Peggy harrumphed as she took her customary seat with her back to the wall, so she was facing the door leading to the main room. 'You think just because a woman uses a cane she needs charity?'

Madge and Carole took their seats, one on either side of Peggy. Baz brought an upholstered chair over from the next table and settled in, facing the window.

A shy grin crossed Daisy's face as she stood back up to her full height. 'I wouldn't dream of it. To be honest, I just really miss our dog back home. I thought maybe it could work out well for all three of us.' She leant back down and smushed his face in her hands. 'Plus, he's just so adorable. How could I resist that face?'

Peggy twisted her lips as she considered the offer. 'I don't let just anyone walk him, you know.'

With her hand still on Cookie's head, Daisy replied, 'And nor should you. You can watch me with him, if you like, to see how I get on.' Cookie looked at Peggy, adding his silent approval to the plan.

Studying Daisy, Peggy wondered what the girl's angle was.

Sarah arrived with a tray of beverages, which she set on the table. Leaving the ladies to sort themselves out, she removed a travel mug from the tray and put it into Daisy's hand before heading back to the shopfront.

Daisy adjusted her rucksack on her shoulder. 'It really was lovely to meet you all. I'll see you at home later, Nan.' She bent and kissed Baz on the cheek then waved at the group before heading back out into the grey morning.

Carole pulled a human heart from her bag and handed it to Cookie. 'Here you go, love.' He lay down under the table to play with it.

Not an actual human heart, of course, though it did resemble one at a casual glance. Peggy smirked as Baz's eyes first widened and then narrowed. The soft toys were Carole's own creation. She had a whole range of handmade anatomically correct bones and organs that she sold as toys.

Once Cookie was settled, Madge nodded thoughtfully. 'That's a good girl you've got there, Baz. Respectful. I like that in a child.'

Peggy rolled her eyes. 'Madge believes in that old claptrap about children being seen and not heard. And don't bother telling her Daisy's not a child. In Madge's view, everyone younger than herself is a child. If you're very lucky, she may excuse you from that. But only on a good day.'

Madge scowled at Peggy before facing Baz. 'Don't listen to her, dear.'

Peggy opened her laptop and re-read the last words she'd written.

'Can we please try not to get into a bit of trouble today?'

'Evie, my dear, trouble is inevitable.' Sam drew closer, just because.

Peggy was pulled back to the café by the sound of Baz chuckling. 'Daisy is indeed a good kid. In fact, she's the reason I moved back here after all these years. She came to live with me and my ... my ex ... a few years ago, back when she first ... well, she had some trouble with her parents. My son, Jason, has a good head on his shoulders ... but not enough heart. Anyways, she was ready for university at the same time as I was looking for a fresh start, so here we are. She's just started at Goldsmiths. For design. The one where, um... That one we were talking about yesterday.'

No one would call Baz a particularly beautiful woman, but she beamed with pride while speaking of her granddaughter. She glowed with an inner beauty. Peggy cursed herself for allowing such sentimental drivel to take root in her mind, her beautifully dark mind.

Madge nodded in approval as she poured a steaming red fluid from her teapot into a china teacup. She leant back and took a sip. 'Now. What have we learnt about this sexual deviant preying upon our community?'

Peggy knew the routine, so she looked at Baz. 'Madge asks a question like that only when she already has an answer. She'll want to speak first and it'll be getting right up her nose that I'm cutting into her time by telling you this.' She raised her mug to her lips but before she drank she added, 'Just so's you know.'

Baz looked like she was trying to stifle a grin.

Madge sucked air through her teeth. 'If you are quite finished, Peggy.'

Peggy took a perverse amount of pleasure in taking a slow sip of her espresso before responding. 'Of course, my dear. Please go ahead and enlighten us.' Espresso really should be drunk in one go but it was worth it just to watch Madge squirm.

Crossing her arms over her chest, Madge looked at the others. 'Well, I spoke to Laura, who spoke to Shannon, who spoke to Nuala, who spoke to Colin. And she told me a young woman from the estate was attacked about four months ago.

Frank's daughter. You remember Frank, don't you, Peggy? They think she was the first. A man followed her as she got off the bus, just like that overly talkative child told us yesterday. At first she thought he was just walking the same direction but when she turned onto Heston Street, so did he.'

Carole opened her knitting bag and began removing items, placing them on her lap. Three skeins of very different yarns, a selection of needles, a half-finished femur, and a new project that could be anything. 'It's like Mickey Mouse and Minnie Mouse. You know Mallorca and Minorca, right? Well, that's all just a metaphor for Napoleon. He was Oberon, and she was his Titania.' She turned to Baz. 'Of course, I'm sure you know it wasn't just a story – it was actually about Napoleon. It's all just mad, isn't it?' She studied the items on her lap, before selecting the new project. She began knitting the teal yarn, adding to ... whatever it was.

It often amused Peggy to observe how people who didn't know Carole reacted to her. But Baz gave just the barest flinch at that. Well, that was no fun.

Madge pulled her reading glasses down her nose and glared at Carole over the top of them. But not too harshly. Madge had a soft spot for Carole. 'As I was saying—'

But she didn't get any further than that because just then a slight Asian man ducked through the door and called out a cheerful, 'Wagwan, ladies?' The Jamaican greeting was relatively common in this part of London – and both Clive and Madge liked to remind people that, however much they both sounded like they were from *sarf London*, both were actually Jamaican.

Madge sucked air through her teeth with just a bit more vim and vigour than usual. 'Wagwan, Clive?'

Peggy felt her lip curl into a sneer. 'Say what you want, Clive.'

Clive clutched his hand to his chest. 'What? Can't a

gentleman come to check up on his favourite local crafting circle?'

'Can't even shout. Can't even cry. The gentlemen are coming by.' Carole sang the words without glancing up from her knitting.

'We are not,' Peggy spoke with ice in her words, 'your favourite local crafting circle, Clive. We're probably not even your seventeenth favourite local crafting circle. And you are not a gentleman.'

'Yes, well. Be that as it may...' Clive's eyes slid greasily off her and over to Baz. 'And who is this lovely creature? You must be new in the area, my dear. Perhaps I can take you out sometime, show you around?'

Madge made an impatient shooing gesture. 'Be off with you. Can't you see we're trying to have a private conversation here?'

Clive smirked, like the arrogant prick he was. 'You're trying to have a hush-hush chat? In this public setting?' He winked at Baz.

Madge reached out with a knitting needle and smacked Clive on the knee. 'Oi. Quit pestering my friend.'

Raising his hands to chest level to deflect blame, then letting his wrists fall limp, Clive looked Baz in the eye. 'I meant no harm.'

Peggy enunciated as clearly as possible, pausing between each word. 'What do you want, Clive?'

'Well.' He bent down and picked up Carole's crocheted femur off the table. Studying it, a grimace crossed his face. 'I wanted to be sure you know about the craft fair coming up. The Purly Queens are hosting it. In the Market Yard. You might be able to make a bit of coin from your ... wares.' He waved the bone around a bit before setting it back on the table. 'Whatever it is you ladies make.' He wiped his hands together as though brushing dust off himself.

Losing patience with the insufferable man, Peggy hoisted herself up from her seat. 'As it happens, Clive, the ladies already make money by selling their works here in this very shop. And online. As do you. Now if you'll excuse me' – she turned to her friends – 'refills?'

When they had all answered, she plucked up her cane and headed for the other room. Cookie lifted his head but when she waved at him to stay, he returned his focus to his heart.

———

BY THE TIME Peggy returned a few moments later, Clive was just leaving. 'That man is infuriating,' she said loudly enough for him to hear just before the door closed behind him.

Madge dropped her elbows to her sides and let out an exasperated-sounding sigh. 'You sleep with a man one time. One time! And he becomes obsessed. The man just cannot get enough of me.'

Peggy glanced over at Baz to see if she reacted to this news but all she showed was a bit of mild curiosity.

'I suppose he's been part of the local community for decades, has he?' Baz asked.

Peggy shook her head. 'He runs the Purly Queens, a local crafters' group. Only arrived a few months ago. What was it – six months? A year?'

Picking her knitting back up, Madge said, 'Not a year. Few months. Must've been April when he arrived. I first met him at the Easter service.'

Peggy looked at the last words she had typed on her screen.

Sam was not like the flowers in the garden that could be put in brackets of where they belonged no matter how rare they were because there was no one like Sam.

Aloud she said, 'I thought you had a bit of a spring in your step that week? Didn't I say so at the time?'

Madge nodded her head. 'Fun was had by all participants.' Baz looked like she'd swallowed something sour what with how hard she was trying not to titter. 'But after both occasions, I found he wouldn't leave me alone.'

Peggy arched an eyebrow at her friend. 'I'm not sure whether my hearing's fading or my memory. But I thought you said it only happened one time, dear.'

Sucking air through her teeth, Madge shook her head. 'Once? Twice? No more than a few.'

Peggy winked at Baz. 'Now, Madge. Before the interruption, you were telling us something. What was it?'

Madge squished up her face in that way she always did when she was pretending to be annoyed. 'I didn't think anybody wanted to hear it.'

Peggy closed her laptop – well, partially closed it. Not enough to put the blasted thing to sleep. 'I assure you, there is nothing I'm looking forward to more.'

Baz furrowed her brow at Peggy, as if to chide her for her sarcasm, before turning to Madge. 'Well, I for one want to know what happened next. The young woman, Frank's daughter, was it? What happened?'

Mollified by Baz's words, Madge peered down her nose over her glasses. 'So, as I was saying, the young lady got off the bus in front of the Albert and then this reprobate followed her up Florence Road, onto Heald Street, and then turned with her onto Heston. Now there's not much on Heston – just a few houses and the back of Pitman.'

She stretched a hand out towards Baz. 'That's the tall block just up the way from here. The miscreant grabbed the girl just as she was passing the old car park. He had a bit of a fondle – but was interrupted by a group of youngsters coming around the corner. She kicked her attacker in the shins and ran for home.'

'My lasses would have done a whole lot more than kick him, I'll tell you that much,' said Carole. Peggy patted her on the knee.

Baz appeared rapt. 'Did she report it?'

'Report it?' Peggy scoffed. 'You think the police are going to do something about a man touching up a young woman on the street? I'll tell you how much resourcing they're going to apply to a case such as that: precisely zero.'

'If you would let me get a word in edgeways,' said Madge. She carried on knitting for a moment. 'As it happens, she did report it. But when the police reviewed the CCTV footage, they said it didn't look like an attack; they thought they were witnessing an argument between people who already knew one another. They filed the report – but as near as the family could tell, they never did anything with it.'

Baz nodded. 'I suppose there's not much they can do about that particular situation. But when it becomes part of a larger pattern, it adds weight to the case against the perpetrator, if you see what I mean.'

'Well, she didn't just report it to the police,' said Madge. 'The folks from the residents association encouraged her to make an ASB report to the housing authority.'

'ASB?' Baz leant forwards. 'What's that?'

'The useless clods at the housing authority keep a log of

antisocial behaviour on the estate.' Peggy opened her computer back up. 'For all the good it does.'

'So they've got a record of it too.' Baz nodded.

Madge cleared her throat. 'Yes, assuming they haven't filed it under gardening requests or just passed it on to the poor caretakers to deal with. But anyhow, that was the first thing I found out. But not the only thing.'

Sarah ducked through the doorway with another tray of drinks. 'Sorry for the wait. It's been quite a busy morning.'

Baz pulled herself up and took the tray from her. 'Thank you, dear. I can deal with that.' Peggy didn't have Madge's ability to pinpoint a person's past injuries, but even she noticed Baz put most of her weight on her left leg, not her right.

Sarah handed her the tray with a smile. Baz laid the various drinks out on the table and then popped through to the other room to return the tray.

As she settled back into her seat, Baz looked up at Madge expectantly. 'So? What else did you learn?'

Crossing her arms over her ample bosom, Madge said, 'Well,' drawing the word out for far too many beats – in a way Peggy's editor would have given her grief over. 'I spoke to young Peter last night. Had him round mine for dinner after he got off shift.' Turning to Baz, she added, 'Young Peter's a copper, works out of the local nick down in Lewisham.'

'Pigs,' proclaimed Carole.

Madge fired her a look that could have wilted her own prized rose bush.

'Peter's a lovely boy, though,' added Carole. 'Hardly tainted at all yet.'

Madge nodded at the first statement and disregarded the second. 'Such a good boy, he is. Now anyhow, over dinner I asked him. Said I'd heard about a scoundrel on the loose and had he heard anything.'

'And what'd he say?' Baz clearly couldn't constrain her curiosity.

Madge, never one to pass up an opportunity, waved in the direction of the teapot. 'Pour me some of that, would you, dear?' Baz did as she was bid as Madge continued her tale. 'Young Peter walks the beat. You'll see him round here quite often. My point is, he's not the one taking reports. He does hear things, though, mind. So's I asked him what he'd heard.'

She picked up her teacup and took a few sips. 'Now, young Peter said he's heard of a few complaints that have been brought in. But according to what he's heard, the police believe the victims have been *unreliable*.' She kissed her teeth once again. 'His word, not mine. In fact, I called him up on that very word. Said I know his daddy taught him better than that because I certainly taught him better than that.'

Madge certainly knew how to suck her audience in. Peggy chuckled softly to herself despite the bile rising in her throat at the thought of this man terrorising her neighbourhood.

Peggy began typing again.

As the carriage pulled into the naval yard, John spotted Sam and a man in uniform. He'd never cared enough to remember his name. And he assured himself he still didn't care even as the two men leant into each other in a conspiratorial manner.

'And?' Baz was on the edge of her seat. 'What did he say to that?'

'Young Peter said that was the word that had been told to him. The police weren't pursuing the case at this time because they didn't have any *reliable* witnesses.' Madge poured the full force of her considerable disdain into the key word. 'I said, "What do you mean? What's wrong with these girls that their word don't mean nothing to your bosses?"'

'I think we know what they mean,' Peggy ventured. Baz looked at her. The look in her eye made Peggy think she understood too.

'Young Peter mumbled his response under his breath. I asked him to repeat himself three times. Finally, he told me his sergeant said they would struggle to get a conviction in cases where the victim is inebriated. Even if they could find the man, it wouldn't make it to trial based on the evidence they have.'

Peggy slammed her laptop closed with enough force to wake Cookie, who got up and padded over to her – moving around the coffee table for once. 'Sorry, Cookie.' She took his head in her hands and buried her gnarled fingers in his thick fur. 'Victim blaming. I honestly thought we'd left that behind us in the last century.'

Baz hung her head and breathed slowly. After a moment she looked up. 'I'm sorry to say we have not.'

'I still say we ought to—'

Peggy put her hand on Carole's knee. 'Yes, dear. We know what you think.'

'Maybe.' Baz touched a finger to her lips. 'Maybe Carole's not entirely wrong, though. Perhaps the cops just need a bit of a helping hand on this one. If we talk to people, gather some evidence, figure out who the perp is ... then maybe the cops will have to act.'

Huh. Maybe this new youngster wasn't all bad. Perhaps she could fit in with their group after all.

CHAPTER 4

in which we discover the extent of baz's culinary skills

BAZ WAS DETERMINED to make the evening perfect – to make a good impression. When the buzzer rang, she was just putting the finishing touches on her cakes. She scuttled to the hall and lifted the buzzer-phone. 'Hello? Spencer residence.'

They'd arrived already. Good. Baz appreciated punctuality. She asked the concierge to send them up and then spent the next few minutes bustling about the place, trying to make sure everything was exactly how she wanted.

After a few minutes, there was a knock at the door. Baz ran to open it. Well, not so much *ran* as hobbled. Her body wasn't up to running these days.

'My my, isn't this fancy.' Peggy whistled as she stepped in and looked around. She wore the same tartan coat over a faded Skunk Anansie T-shirt over her slender frame. 'We'd have been up here many minutes ago but it turned out the concierge was a school friend of one of Madge's brood.'

'Would you mind just removing your shoes?' Baz tried not to let her grimace show. 'Sorry. It's very Canadian of me. I hope you don't mind.'

Madge nodded approvingly and they all did as requested. Though Peggy did point out that Cookie wore no shoes.

Carole moved with a speed and grace that belied her plump form as she and Cookie made a beeline for the big window with its view out over Deptford and New Cross and further afield to Southwark and even the City. The pair stood side by side, silently staring out. The sun wouldn't set for a couple more hours yet, but it was already visible in the western distance.

'Good evening, Baz.' Madge removed a light overcoat, which Baz took and hung up in the hall cupboard. 'Did you know Jessica – that's the name of the child down there at the front desk... She's friends with my Julie's eldest, Tyson. They were at Addey & Stanhope together – the school just the other side of the estate, on New Cross Road. Young Tyson's lady friend has recently blessed me with my third great-grandbaby. I was showing Jessica some photos.'

Peggy followed Carole over to the window. She peered out for a few seconds, nodded, and took a seat on the sofa with her back to the wall. 'Madge, she's not interested in a potted history of your clan. Just tell her what you've been dying to.'

Carole turned from the window and faced the group. 'It was such a shame about New York in 1922. But then they built it all back up again by 1956.'

'That's nice, love. Come and take a seat.' Peggy patted the sofa next to herself. Carole walked over, brushed the sofa with her hands, and sat down.

Madge continued to stand at the edge of the open-plan living-room-kitchen-diner space. 'Do you know that child's only job is to keep an eye on things going on in the neighbourhood?'

'Well, I wouldn't have put it that way.' Baz stopped talking when she saw the look in Madge's eye. Noticing that the older woman wasn't coming any further into the flat, Baz motioned for her to join the rest of the group. 'Please come in. Make yourself at home. Sit anywhere you like.'

Making a circuit of the room, Madge continued her tale. 'So, I asked Jessica about our menace, thinking she may know more than the local plod.' She coughed. 'Sorry, my throat's very dry.'

Baz raised her hands in alarm. 'Of course, of course! Where are my manners? Now, I have wine – a good selection of Canada's finest. But I've also got some juices, tea, coffee, and of course water.'

Peggy arched an eyebrow. 'Wine? From Canada? What's it made from? Surely it's too cold to grow grapes.'

Baz allowed a grin to spread across her face as she waggled a finger at her friend. 'Ah, now that's where you're wrong, Peggy. What's your poison – white, red, or rosé?'

At Peggy's request, Baz uncorked a bottle of Cabernet Sauvignon from the Okanagan Valley, which Madge also chose. Carole selected a Viognier from Niagara. Baz put out a bowl of water for Cookie and then joined the women.

Once everyone had sampled their beverages and declared them to be drinkable and – in Peggy's case – 'probably from actual grapes', Madge resumed her story.

'Now Jessica told me that she heard from Tiana who works at the hotel that's attached to this building – who heard from their overnight desk clerk... Did you know they have their own separate entrance with their own front desk staff separate from the flats here? Anyhow, this young man told Tiana, who told Jessica, who told me, that a few nights ago he'd spoken to a girl who said—'

'Oh, for pity's sake, Madge! I'm going to die of old age

before you even get to the punchline.' Peggy drained the last of her wine in one long go.

Madge sucked air through her teeth. 'I will get there in my own time.'

Baz made to stand up to get more wine but Peggy waved her down. 'I've got it. You stay here and listen to the retelling of the story. It didn't take half so long to live through it the first time around.'

'Now as I was saying.' Madge sounded put out. 'This child working the front desk at the hotel... What was his name? Luke? Lewis?'

Carole removed her knitting from her bag and started working on it. 'Lukasz.' For all Carole's bizarre talk, Baz couldn't help but notice she certainly had a keen ear for details.

Madge waved at Carole in acknowledgement. 'That's right, Lukasz. So, as I was saying, young Lukasz was working the front desk at the hotel on Monday night when a group of young people came in, shepherding a woman who'd just been attacked. They wanted to know if she could wait there for the police but the girl waved them off. Didn't want police involved.'

Peggy returned from the kitchen with both wine bottles and placed them on the coffee table. Baz topped everyone up while Madge continued her story.

'The poor child was hysterical. Of course Lukasz, who sounds like a good boy, said she could sit in the lobby as long as she needed.'

Baz stopped with her glass just below her lips. 'And then what?' Her heart was racing. What kind of place had she brought Daisy to? What would her family say if they found out what was happening? They already resented her – if she'd placed Daisy in danger... She fought off a shudder.

Madge held her hands up in front of herself. 'That was as much as Jessica knew.'

The conversation fell into a lull for a few seconds until Baz took a sharp intake of breath and leapt to her feet – and instantly grimaced as pain shot through her knee. 'Dinner!' She toddled to the kitchen as quickly as her wounded body would carry her, followed by the others.

Baz released the steam valve on her pressure cooker, which fired a juicy geyser of toxic-smelling vapours up to the ceiling. 'Oh dear.' She waved a hand ineffectually at the device, attempting to dissipate the steam.

She hobbled to the smoke detector to slam the blasted thing off just as it declared, 'Emergency. There's smoke in the kitchen.' Making to unclamp the lid of the pressure cooker, she decided better of it. And broke down in tears instead.

Carole ran to the balcony, sliding the door open to bring in some air. Madge opened all the windows she could see. Which left Peggy to console the sobbing Baz.

Awkwardly patting her new friend's back, Peggy said, 'There, there.'

Stifling a giggle, Baz wiped a tear with her sleeve. Given what she knew of Peggy, those were probably the only comforting words she knew.

Peggy filled the kettle and flicked it on before rummaging through cupboards, muttering to herself. Baz looked up through glassy eyes, puzzled. 'Do you need something?'

'I'm not much for consoling. Normally when there are tears, I just make the … the … afflicted individual a cup of tea. Preferably in a nice, big, bowl-shaped mug. I place it in their hands and then back away slowly.'

Baz blinked a few times. 'Bless you, dear. And, yes, a cup of tea would be perfect. The teabags are in that cupboard there.' She flung a hand out to indicate the relevant cupboard – only for her hand to crash into Madge's breast. With a squeal, Baz ran from the room to have a good cry in the privacy of her bathroom, leaving her guests untended. For the past few months, it felt like she came undone at the slightest thing.

What must they think of her? Surely they'd give up on her now that it was apparent how utterly useless she was. No, she wouldn't let herself give in to a spiral of shame and self-loathing.

Once she'd begun transitioning, she'd gradually stopped seeing all her friends. It wasn't that they rejected her. In fact, they'd all been lovely – shocked perhaps, but after a day or so they'd all adapted. They'd been very polite. Using her new name and respecting her pronouns. No one laughed or did anything awful.

And yet, she'd felt awkward around them. They hadn't rejected her – she'd rejected herself on their behalf.

Terrified of making the same mistake again with her new friends, Baz dried her eyes and blew her nose. She poked her head out the door once more. Creeping as quietly as she could, she made her way back down the hall to the living room, where she found her friends gathered around Peggy's laptop.

'I'm sorry I ruined dinner. It's the hormones, I think. And life and everything – sometimes I just get completely overwhelmed.'

Peggy clicked a few more buttons before standing upright and stretching out her back. 'Never you mind about that. It's all sorted. Dinner will be here in forty minutes.'

'Oh.' Baz looked at the floor. 'That's good, I guess. I am sorry, ladies. Daisy left me a recipe and I thought she'd made a typo on the time. That there was no way it could cook so fast. I should have known better.' She shook her head. 'I've made a real hash of this – haven't I?'

'Nonsense,' said Madge. 'Happens to everyone.'

Feeling a weight beginning to lift off her shoulders, Baz wiped her eyes again. 'Does it?'

Madge waved a hand. 'Not me, of course. But everybody else.'

'Of course.' Baz bit back a small laugh. 'What are we having, then?'

'Curry.' Peggy put her cane down firmly on the wood floor. 'Everyone loves curry.'

'Perfect.' Baz nodded – she'd been trying to make chana saag anyways. 'Oh! I have an idea.' She made her way to the kitchen and removed her cake from its hiding spot in the oven. 'I may not be able to cook – but I do like to bake. What say we treat ourselves to a bit of dessert while we wait for the main to arrive?'

Madge elbowed Peggy in the ribs. 'I told you I liked this one – didn't I?'

Peggy rolled her eyes.

Baz went to dish up the cakes. Lifting the lid, she said, 'I had another idea as well.'

Peggy and Madge exchanged glances. 'And what might that be?' Peggy asked.

'After dinner, I wondered if perhaps we might all go and have a chat with Lukasz – see what he knows about this predator on the loose in our community?'

Madge grinned. 'What a lovely idea. It's a shame I didn't think of it.'

———

Two hours later, sated and only slightly tipsy, the four women headed down to the hotel to chat with Lukasz. The hotel adjoined Baz's building, so the trip from one to the other took only a handful of seconds.

It turned out Peggy had a mobility scooter as well. Baz figured she must live quite close to the café, as she'd never noticed another one parked there. Their normal positions were reversed – Baz walked with a cane and Peggy steered her scooter out the door of Baz's building and around the corner to the hotel entrance.

When the door slid open, a young man with a round face and blond hair looked up and smiled. 'Good evening, ladies? Checking in, are we?'

'What a lovely child.' Madge looked at her friends. 'Such nice manners.' She walked up to the front desk and placed her hands on it.

'As it happens,' said Peggy, joining Madge at the front desk, 'we are not checking in.'

'We're here to talk to you.' Madge raised her glasses to her face and squinted at the man's name tag. 'Lukasz.'

Lukasz practically squealed in delight – feigned or otherwise. 'Oh my. Four of you and only one of me. How exciting! What shall we talk about?'

'Don't be flippant.' Peggy put one hand on her hip. Cookie promptly sat down. Baz wondered whether it was a coincidence or if the hand on the hip was a signal Peggy had taught him.

Baz joined her friends at the counter. 'As lovely as I'm sure it would be to chat with you about nothing in particular, we're actually here to talk about the incident on Monday night.'

The smile melted off Lukasz's face and he adopted a sombre pose. 'The incident?'

Baz fought the urge to remove a non-existent notebook and pen from her non-existent pocket. 'On Monday night, we understand a woman was brought in here by a group of young people.'

Apparently, Madge had no such compunction. She opened her enormous handbag and removed a hardback notebook and pen. Licking her finger and flipping pages, she found the one she wanted and looked up at Lukasz expectantly.

Lukasz swallowed and tugged on his ear. 'You're cops? You're not cops. Are you?'

Madge pulled herself up to her full height. 'No. We're merely four harmless old ladies who are concerned about the safety of our community. If someone is preying on youngsters in our area, we want to ensure something is done about it. You understand?'

Lukasz nodded. 'Yes, ma'am.' He cleared his throat. 'What do you want to know?'

Carole took Cookie's lead from Peggy's hand and walked over to the grey and yellow sofas at the far end of the space. Madge and Peggy both looked to Baz, seemingly satisfied that she should know best how to question a witness – which wasn't entirely true. Her career as a civilian investigator with the RCMP had mostly involved poring over documents and spreadsheets, not questioning people.

Baz took a step closer to the desk, wishing she'd not had that last glass of wine. Or possibly that she'd had more. 'Do you recall the incident we're speaking of?'

'Yes, s— ma'am.' Lukasz nodded.

'When was this?'

Lukasz closed his eyes for a second. 'Monday night.'

Baz leant against the tall reception desk. 'This past Monday, you mean?' Another nod. 'Do you recall what time it was?'

Lukasz appeared to think about the question for a bit. 'Ah, let me just check something.' He began tapping keys on his computer. He watched the screen for a few seconds before looking back up. 'They came in at 23:37.' He clicked a few more keys. 'The whole group remained until the sister arrived and collected the young woman just before midnight.'

Baz felt her breath catch. 'I don't suppose you'd let us have a little peek at that CCTV footage, would you?'

'Much as I adore having the attention of four lovely ladies, I won't risk my job for you.' Lukasz winked. 'I'll answer questions where I can ... but that's as far as it goes.'

Madge nodded approvingly. 'That's all we're asking, honey. Just a little chat.'

'All we want is to keep our community safe,' Peggy said.

Baz looked at the other two but they seemed to be waiting for her to continue her questions. 'So, Lukasz.'

Lukasz nodded. He really was a very handsome young man.

'Can you tell us what happened, please? Start from the moment the door opened. What did you see? What did you hear? Tell us everything you remember.'

Looking up to the ceiling, Lukasz said, 'I had just finished checking in a guest when the door opened again. Two men brought a woman in.'

Madge scribbled furiously in her notebook.

Baz touched her chin. 'When you say they brought her in – what do you mean? Were they carrying her or just walking together?'

'They were supporting her. Each of them had an arm around her. She was crying. I asked how I could help but one of them motioned for me to wait a minute. They ushered her over there' – he gestured to the seating area where Carole and Cookie waited – 'and then one stayed with her while the other came and talked to me. He said they'd been walking towards the station through Broadway Fields. You know the park behind us, yes?'

The three women nodded and Lukasz continued his story. 'They'd heard a girl screaming and they'd chased her attacker off. He told me they were pretty sure she'd been raped but the girl wasn't ... she wasn't all that coherent, you know? And maybe her English isn't so good.'

Lukasz swallowed. 'I dialled 999 and asked for police and ambulance. They said I had to choose just one service to route my call to but before I could, the woman was wailing and screaming. She ran over here and begged me to hang up. I apologised to the operator and said I'd call again later if it was appropriate.'

He raised a hand to his mouth and Baz thought he might be fighting back tears. 'She was... What's the right word? Distraught, I think. We all wanted to help − but she just wanted to go home. She made that much clear. "No police. No ambulance. Home. Sister." In the end, she called her sister and I made her a cup of tea while she waited.'

Peggy pointed a finger at Madge. 'See? I told you tea was the answer.'

Madge shushed her and Lukasz continued his story. 'The lads stayed with her until the sister arrived. One of them had a quick chat with the sister outside before she came in. I'm not sure what he said to her, though. Anyway, her sister took her home and that was the last I saw of her.'

Baz nodded thoughtfully. 'I don't suppose you got contact details for any of them, did you?'

Lukasz tilted his head slightly. 'I think one of the blokes gave his number to the sister. But I don't have it.'

Madge wrote her number down in her notebook and tore the corner of the page out. 'In case you remember anything else.' She held the number out to Lukasz and then withdrew it. 'Now don't you be calling me for any purposes other than this. I appreciate a younger man ... but you're a touch too young even for me. So don't get any ideas in that head of yours.' She winked as she slid the paper across the counter to him.

Lukasz coloured as he studied the paper. The women bade him goodbye and then headed back out into the night.

As her guests made to leave, Baz remembered something. 'Oh, good heavens. I never did tell you.' She touched her hand to her forehead.

'Tell us what, dear?' Peggy eyed her suspiciously.

'The real reason I first approached you in Wellbeloved.'

Madge waved the idea away. 'It's gone nine already. You can tell us in the morning.'

CHAPTER 5

in which baz makes a confession

WHEN BAZ and Daisy arrived at Wellbeloved the next morning, the other ladies were just walking down Tanner's Hill. Daisy waved while Baz parked her mobility scooter.

'Morning, ladies,' Daisy called out. 'And good morning, Cookie.' The dog loped as far ahead of Peggy as his lead would let him, eager to greet his new favourite human. After fussing over him for a few seconds, Daisy looked up, using her left hand to shield her eyes from the bright sunlight. 'What do you think, Peggy? Are you okay to supervise me walking him for a few minutes?'

'You're not going to give an old woman any peace until she concedes, are you?' Peggy's words were harsh, but she had a wry grin as she handed over the lead.

Baz touched Daisy's shoulder as she passed. 'We'll meet you inside, okay?' But Daisy only had eyes for Cookie.

It was a chilly morning and Baz was grateful for the warm, aromatic atmosphere of the café. They placed their orders and headed for their usual seats. Baz took off her coat and draped it over the back of her chair before sitting.

Once the group were settled, Madge bent down to collect her knitting from her bag. 'Well?'

Carole leant back in her chair. 'My Tina threw a suitor down a well once. I wonder if they ever found his body. You'd think I'd have heard something by now.'

Still facing Baz, Madge shifted her eyes to Carole. 'Not now, dear. Baz has some explaining to do.'

Baz took a deep breath. 'Can we wait for Peggy, please? I promise I'll tell you everything.' Much as she didn't want to prolong her own agony, it was only fair to make her confession with the whole group present.

Madge frowned. 'I suppose.' She smoothed her knitting project out and studied it for a moment before picking her needles up.

Baz pulled her new embroidery project from her bag. First thing this morning, she'd opened all the supplies and got started so her friends wouldn't see her struggle. She'd spent the past few days watching YouTube tutorials and getting herself reacquainted with what to do.

As Baz made the first few stitches, the silence felt awkward. She was sure she could hear herself swallowing, her heart beating, a clock somewhere ticking. A child playing in the next room. The hiss of the machinery as Sarah made coffees.

After a few minutes, Sarah brought over a tray of drinks and placed them on the table. She seemed to sense something was amiss. 'Mum?' She put her hands on her hips. 'Is everything okay?'

Holding her lips tight, Madge looked up. 'We shall see.'

Carole looked Sarah in the eye and smiled brightly. 'They mix up central heating with cheating. When in fact, it's actually the internet passing through Bastille.'

Sarah, clearly accustomed to these Caroleisms, touched her

shoulder gently. 'You'll let me know if you need anything else, yeah?'

'Mmm hmm,' muttered Madge.

Baz put on a cheerful, optimistic face. 'Thank you.'

Sarah's eyes roved from woman to woman. 'Well, all right then. You know where to find me if you need me.' She ducked back through the doorway just as the front door opened. 'Morning, ladies,' she said to Peggy and Daisy. She gave Cookie a quick pat on the head.

'Congratulations on successfully observing both the time of day and our shared gender,' said Peggy, causing Sarah to grin and shake her head as she made her way back to the front counter.

'Well.' Madge studied Daisy and then looked at Peggy. 'How'd the child do?'

'She did fine. Even had Cookie sit when they got to the corner.'

Daisy beamed with pride. 'I've only got one class on Fridays. If you like, I can come back in a couple hours? Maybe take him to the dog park for a bit?'

Peggy took her seat. 'That would be fine. Cookie enjoys the park. Much more than I do. Those people there – all they do is gossip.'

'Okay, well... I guess I'd better be off. I suppose I'll see you in a few hours.' She bent down to where Cookie had lay down next to Peggy and addressed him directly. 'And you, save up your energy because we're going to the P-A-R-K in a bit.' After collecting her coffee mug from the table, she practically bounced out of the café.

The moment the door closed behind Daisy, Peggy turned to Madge. 'Well, did you squeeze the truth out of her yet or did you hold her over the hot coals until I got here?'

'We decided to wait until you arrived,' said Madge.

Baz had been steeling herself for this confession for several days. And yet now that it was time, her stomach was doing backflips. All her resolve had melted away. 'Okay. See, well, the thing is...'

'Oh good heavens. Skip to the end already, would you?' Peggy picked up her espresso and downed it in one.

Baz swallowed. 'It's about my Daisy, you see.' Deep breath. 'She's not had an easy life. When she came out to her parents ... to my son and that shrew of a woman he married...' She wiped a tear from her eye. 'I promised myself I wouldn't cry.'

'It's okay.' Madge fired a look at Peggy. 'Take your time.'

Baz poured herself some tea from the pot in front of her, steadying her nerves. 'My son ... I think there's a good person somewhere inside him. But he was raised mostly by his mother. And he inherited her worldview. So when Daisy came out at the age of fifteen, he gave her a choice – go back in that closet or leave. My husband and I opened our home to her. She's lived with me ever since.'

The bell over the front door jangled again, and a familiar figure appeared. Instead of going to the front counter to order, Clive sashayed straight towards the women. 'Ladies.'

Madge inhaled slowly. 'Clive.'

Peggy ground her teeth. 'What are you doing here, Clive?'

'Oh, I meant to ask.' Carole raised her head and looked directly at Clive. 'Do you still play the game of magenta?'

'I'm afraid I don't know that one, dear.' Clive touched his chest. 'What is it?'

'You're an idiot.' Carole went back to her crocheting.

Clive shook his head. 'Anyhoo... Wagwan, ladies? I just popped in for some coffee. Thought I should say hello while I was here.' He reached out to touch Madge's knitting project but she slapped his hand. He tsked. 'Alrighty then. I'll see you ladies around.'

When he'd gone, Madge glared over the top of her glasses. 'I bet it's him.'

'What's him?' Baz tilted her head.

'The one we're looking for.' Madge's needles continued their click-clack rhythm.

'You think he's the' – Baz's jaw dropped – 'the ... the local predator?'

'Wouldn't surprise me.'

Peggy scoffed. 'Nor me. Knowing him.'

Madge fixed Baz with a stare. 'Carry on, then.'

Baz took a long drink of her tea, determined not to let herself cry. She tried to remember where she'd left off. 'Inspired by Daisy's courage, I began to question some things about myself. Around a year ago, just before my accident, I decided I owed it to myself to transition. I won't go into everything that followed but Hari – that's my husband – left. Daisy remained with me. She's been my one constant over the past few years and I've been hers. Everything I do is for her.'

Setting her teacup back on the table, she looked at the others. Madge's face was passive, neutral. Carole was away with the fairies.

Peggy looked annoyed but waved Baz's concerns off. 'This face is for the people who did you and Daisy wrong. I'm reserving judgement on you until you get to the point of all this.'

Cookie crawled under the low table until his face poked out by Baz's knees. He sniffed at her, then squeezed himself the rest of the way out. He stood up, turned around twice, and sat down, leaning into her legs.

Placing her hand on Cookie's head, Baz continued. 'When she finished high school, she did a gap year, working to save up money. Later, with the settlement I got from my accident, I could have paid for her university but she's still adamant she wants to contribute.'

Madge nodded. 'She's a hard worker. I can respect that.'

Baz picked her tea back up. 'She is. And when she was looking at universities, she considered a few. But she wanted a fresh start. And she said I deserved one too. And it just so happens that Goldsmiths is one of the best places in the world for design – which is what she wanted to study. So we're here. And now...'

She dabbed at her eyes with a serviette. 'She met someone a few days after we arrived – so this would have been almost a month ago. Right from the off, I didn't like him. Oh, he's very smooth. Charming. But I could tell there was something not quite right about him. I know you shouldn't judge people ... but I knew. And sure enough, one week into the relationship, he asked for money.'

Peggy's painted eyebrow shot up and Madge stopped knitting.

'Not much at first. Just twenty quid. And Daisy's all heart, so she gave him what he said he needed. And then the next day, he said he was behind on child support and his ex could use it to stop him seeing his kids. This time he needed £120. I knew then that this was never going to stop. I told her if she paid it, the next request would be in the thousands. But Daisy always wants to believe the best in people.'

'Someone tried that with my Diane once.' Carole tittered. 'Idiot. No one makes that mistake twice.'

Baz fought back both a chuckle and a tear. 'Daisy can protect herself physically. I'm not worried about her in that regard. But emotionally...' She balanced her tea carefully on the arm of the chair for a moment as she wiped away a tear. 'Last weekend, he told her his ex was on the verge of being evicted from her home. His kids were going to be sleeping on the street unless she could come up with £2,500 before the end of the day.'

Peggy slapped the keyboard of her computer. 'This chancer expected that lovely young woman to pay his ex-partner's rent? I'll break his arm myself.'

Baz took a sip of her tea. 'He assured her he was divorced from the ex and the last thing he wanted was to be paying her rent. But...'

'Won't somebody please think of the children?' The amount of scorn Peggy poured into her words was enough to take out a herd of elephants.

Baz released a long, slow breath. 'Got it in one. I urged her not to pay but she was adamant about helping. Thankfully, she's not entirely without sense. She told him she'd get in touch with the housing authority and arrange to pay them directly.'

Madge nodded approvingly. Peggy clapped in delight. 'Clever girl!'

'Indeed. Of course, he fought and he argued. He tried to charm his way out of it. He offered her the phone number of "his contact"' – Baz made rabbit ears around the relevant phrase – 'at the housing authority and told her to call him directly. He made a thousand and one excuses for why she shouldn't just hand the money straight to the local council.'

Cookie pawed at Baz's hand, so she rubbed his soft face. 'When he finally figured out she wasn't going to hand the money over, he vanished. Just *poof*, gone.' She shook her head. 'Poor girl's heartbroken.'

Silence fell over the group like a warm blanket. Peggy clicked the keys of her laptop. Madge undid a row of her knitting project. Carole carried on working on what appeared to be a crocheted model of a human leg bone. Baz could feel her heart in her throat. She focused on Cookie's face and tried to quell her rising sense of panic.

'I'm sorry that happened to Daisy,' said Peggy. 'It's good she's free of that scoundrel. But I'm sorry it happened.' She looked Baz in the eye, like she was studying for an exam. 'What I'm not clear on is what this has to do with you initiating conversation with us.'

Peggy and Madge exchanged a look.

Baz nodded. 'After all this happened, I went to the police station. You know, the big one down by the shopping centre?'

'Lewisham nick,' said Peggy at the same time as Carole muttered, 'Filth!'

'I thought maybe I could convince them to look into the guy. With my experience, I don't know, I guess I just thought I could persuade them to have a word with him. Out of professional courtesy, you know? Or something. Anything.' Baz shook her head. 'But they treated me like I was some doddering old woman. They all but patted me on the head and told me not to trouble myself.'

Once again, Peggy and Madge looked at one another. Then Peggy slid her laptop into her bag and leant forwards in her chair. 'I have two questions for you – and I want you to think very carefully before you answer.'

'Okay.' Baz sat up straight.

Peggy looked Baz square in the eye. 'Number one – this fellow is out of Daisy's life now. Based on what you've told us, I doubt he'll be back. So, why are you still interested in the matter?' Baz opened her mouth to reply but Peggy shushed her. 'Let me finish. Second question – why did you decide to bring this matter to *us*? Before you'd even met us, you had clearly decided we could help. Why was that?' She raised a bony finger with its flaked black polish and held it out.

Baz looked out the window for a moment before speaking. 'The first one is easy. I care because even though Daisy is safe from this man's nefarious purposes, others aren't. This scheme of his ... it was very skilfully executed. He knew what he was doing. This can't have been the first time he's done this – and it won't be the last. Daisy's my girl. I'll do anything for her. Anything. But there are other Daisys out there – and maybe they don't have a Baz.'

Peggy nodded. 'Good answer.'

'Mmm hmm,' said Madge.

Folding her hands neatly in her lap, Baz took a deep breath. 'The second one is harder.'

'Nobody gonna rush you,' said Madge.

'The truth is, I'm not entirely sure *why*.' Baz pursed her lips. 'I discovered this coffee shop one day while out for a walk and I saw you ladies sitting here and... I can't honestly say. Not entirely.'

Baz poured the rest of her tea into her cup, added a splash of oat milk and stirred. 'One day last week when I came in here, I overheard you organising things for a young family who'd lost their home in a fire. I didn't hear everything that went on, but you were bringing the community together to arrange help for them. It just seemed to me like you were the sort of women who get stuff done.'

Madge chuckled at that. She and Peggy looked at each other yet again.

'I don't know why I thought you would or even could help. But the more I've got to know you over the past few days... The way I've seen you take on the cause of this sex pest preying on your community – *our* community... It all serves to reinforce the idea that I called it right. You're folks who make things happen.'

Baz pricked her finger with her embroidery needle. 'Well, there's that and the other side of it is that I've just been so lonely. All my old friends in Canada ... well, it's just been awkward with them since I transitioned. None of them were

49

horrible about it – not at all. But I just felt awkward around them. And then we moved here and I've been all alone. Except for Daisy, I mean. I wanted to make some friends and you seemed like the sort of people who might ... who might...' The tears threatened to overwhelm her again.

Carole threw down her crochet project and smiled cheerily. 'I forgot to mention! I found out what the genesis tapes are.'

Although Baz was still unsure how best to respond to Carole sometimes, she was grateful for the distraction. 'Oh. And what are they?'

Carole's face darkened as she scowled at Baz. 'Don't you patronise me, young lady.' But then she brightened again. 'And would you believe it – the dentists and the Portuguese are in it together. They tell you you've got an impacted wisdom tooth and you have to go to the homeopathic hospital, but then they really put a tape recorder round your neck. It's all just mad, isn't it?'

'Oh. Okay.'

Peggy leant forwards and took Carole's hand in her own. 'We're in the coffee shop, love. When you're ready to join us...'

Carole turned to face her. 'I'll be there as soon as I can, dear. Shouldn't be too much longer. Thanks for calling.' She picked her project back up and resumed her work.

Sitting back upright, Peggy turned to face Baz once again. 'As you've seen over the past few days, we ... are keen supporters of our community. And you are part of that community. As is Daisy.'

Madge peered over the top of her glasses. 'So that leaves us with one question. Is this fellow a local? Or was this some sort of computer scam?'

Baz felt her heart soar. She knew they'd understand. 'Oh, he's local all right.' She tilted her head, considering the matter. 'Or, at least, I assume so. He sounds local and she met him in the neighbourhood. That cocktail bar down by the train station.'

Peggy furrowed her brow. 'Under the station? Or near it?'

'Under.'

Madge nodded. 'Little Nan's. We like that place.'

Peggy hoisted herself up out of her chair, causing Cookie to stand up too. 'No, you lie back down, mister. I'm just going to the loo.' To the others, she added, 'Very good for an afternoon tipple. Madge, you get the details out of her while I'm seeing to my needs. I'll get another round of beverages as well, shall I? And when I'm back, I'll make reservations for afternoon tea tomorrow.'

Everyone nodded, except Cookie, who picked up his toy and crawled under the low table with it.

'So.' Madge's eyes bored into Baz's soul. 'Tell us everything you know about this rake.'

CHAPTER 6

in which we learn of the pornstar nan

THE MARKET WAS in full swing as the ladies walked – or, in Peggy and Baz's case, rolled – down Deptford High Street. Traders from various stalls cried out their greetings and a few came from under the shelter of their marquees to fuss over Cookie. Much as Peggy wished they'd all leave her alone, she knew Cookie deserved all the attention he received, so she tried to be patient with people.

'Got some nice cassava for you, Mrs Dixon,' called one man. Madge waved and thanked him.

Someone shouted 'Granny!'

Madge's head swung left and right and back again. 'Oh, I know that voice.' The buildings bounced sound around, making it difficult to tell where the shouter was. The others joined Madge in trying to find the source.

'Over here,' came a different voice.

At last Peggy spotted them. She thumped Madge with her cane. 'That way.' She used the cane to indicate the two police officers taking shelter from the rain under a shop awning – both smiling and waving. 'It's Peter.' She disregarded the fact her movements had almost taken out a young couple.

'Of course it's young Peter.' Madge shoved her way through the crowd to the edge of the pavement, where the officers stood. 'I told you I knew that voice.'

Peggy looked at the two uniformed officers, similar height and build. One had rich mahogany skin and the other had cool beige. They grinned like a pair of idiots.

Madge hugged the Black man to her, before turning to her newest friend. 'Baz, this is my grandson, young Peter. He's a constable with the Met.' Madge released the man and indicated Baz. 'And this is my friend, Ms Barbara Spencer.' She put just enough emphasis on the word *Ms* for everyone to know she didn't approve of it.

Peter smiled. 'Lovely to meet you, Ms Spencer.' He nodded at Carole and Peggy. 'Aunties.'

Peggy nodded her head cordially. 'Peter.' Carole, on the other hand, appeared to strike up a conversation with a lamp post, refusing to look at the pair.

The white man cleared his throat. He raised the bottle of grapefruit juice he held in one hand and took a swig.

Behind black-framed glasses, Peter's eyes widened. 'Oh, sorry. Ladies, this is my new partner, PC Mike West. He just transferred from Hammersmith a few weeks back. Mike, this is my grandmother, Mrs Dixon. And these are her friends, Ms Trent, Ms Spencer. And that's Mrs Ballard over there, pretending she doesn't know us.' He gestured to where Carole was listening intently to what the lamp post had to say.

PC West flashed a very charming smile accompanied by a set of dimples. 'Charmed, I'm sure. And please ... call me Mike.' Peggy had never been enamoured of men but she imagined people probably found him attractive. 'It's lovely to chat with you ladies but I'm afraid Peter and I must get back to work.' He smiled again. 'Unless there's anything you need our assistance with, of course.'

Peggy suspected many people would fall victim to his charms. 'Not just yet. Not just yet.'

The officer glanced from left to right. 'My, how cryptic. All right. Well, we'll be around when you do need us. You ladies have a good afternoon.' He took another drink from his juice bottle.

Madge licked her finger and smoothed Peter's tight curls and plucked a non-existent piece of lint from his uniform. 'We will. Thank you. You behave yourself, child.'

Poor Peter looked like he wanted to hide under one of the merchant's tables. 'Yes, Granny.'

The ladies resumed their journey and soon arrived at Little Nan's Cocktail Bar. Peggy and Baz parked their scooters outside. The group shook out and closed their umbrellas before heading in. They greeted the bar staff on their way. A table booked in Peggy's name was waiting.

The large railway arch was stuffed to the gills with, well, stuff. It was a riot of bright colours, leopard print, fairy lights, and fake plants. Fabric in conflicting patterns covered almost every square centimetre of the ancient brick walls. Mismatched tables and chairs sat atop a concrete floor covered in well-worn rugs. Bunting and tinsel were layered over the fabric on the walls. A wide array of knick-knacks and trinkets littered every flat surface.

Once she was seated, Baz placed her hands on the arms of her chair. 'Well, ladies. This is all rather lovely, but I'm a bit perplexed. I told you Daisy met her horrible beau at a cocktail bar and you responded by telling me we'd be going for after-noon tea ... and now I find myself in the very same cocktail bar. I don't suppose you'd care to enlighten?'

Before Peggy could answer, the bartender appeared,

carrying a tall, tiered serving platter of dainty scones, finger sandwiches, and cakes, as well as a stack of four small china plates. 'Mrs Dixon, Ms Trent, Mrs Ballard – oh, and you've got a new friend with you today.'

Thunder clapped overhead as Baz introduced herself. 'Lovely to meet you. I'm Barbara Spencer. Please call me Baz.'

'All right, Baz. I'm Kevin.' He placed the food on the table. 'So, ladies, we've got a selection of goodies for you here. And I'll take your drinks order whenever you're ready.'

Peggy gave Baz a deadly serious look. 'Baz, do you trust us?'

Baz paused for a moment and Peggy thought she looked a bit lost. 'Um ... yes?'

'Good, there's my girl.' Peggy clapped her on her good knee before looking up at the bartender. 'We'll have a Lord Paddy Ashdown, please, and a Pornstar Nan.' She glanced outside at the weather and added, 'And given it's not very busy today, we're hoping to ask you a few questions.'

'Ooh, colour me intrigued,' Kevin replied. 'Let me get to work on your drinks and I'll be back over for a little chat.'

'Thank you, Kevin,' Madge said. 'And how's your mum? Has her hip still been giving her grief?'

'Actually, she said to thank you. She asked her GP about that medicine you recommended. Her pain's been much better since starting it. I'll be back in a few.'

'Well, then.' Peggy rubbed her hands together. 'Let's tuck in.'

The next few minutes were spent sampling the wares on the table. Even Cookie got a few little nibbles.

Swallowing her mouthful of scone, Peggy fixed Baz with a look. 'I really must say, Baz... For a veteran cop, you're not very streetwise.'

'Ah, yes about that.' Colour rose in Baz's cheeks. 'It's true that I worked for the police – for forty years, in fact. But I was a civilian investigator. My specialty was large-scale financial crime.' She used her napkin to dab at her lips. 'I'm an accountant, you see.'

Peggy merely smirked but Madge laughed uproariously.

'I suppose I just spent enough time amongst cops to pick up the lingo and, well, the body language.' Baz gave an apologetic shrug.

Kevin returned with two mismatched teapots and set them on the table. 'Shall I fetch cups for you or do you want to pick your own?'

'You can bring them, dear,' said Madge, wiping a bit of cucumber sandwich from the corner of her mouth.

Kevin plucked four cups from the display in the window. Baz appeared to be finding the whole process absolutely delightful – if the childlike glow on her face was anything to go by.

Madge picked up the first teapot and poured a bit into one of the cups. 'Try this one and see how you like it.'

Baz picked the cup up and peered at the chartreuse liquid inside. 'This doesn't look like tea.' She sniffed the contents. 'Hoo! Doesn't smell like it either.'

'It's the only kind of tea worth drinking.' Peggy couldn't abide tea. Now, booze on the other hand ... booze she enjoyed. In moderation, of course.

Baz brought the cup to her lips. Her eyes widened as she drank. She coughed. 'That's powerful stuff.'

Kevin grinned. 'That's the Lord Paddy Ashdown, a whisky cocktail. It's one of my personal favourites. And it's Peggy's go-to tipple.'

Peggy nodded. She had always – well, *almost* always – thought quite highly of Paddy Pantsdown. She'd admired his commitment. And the cocktail named in his honour couldn't be beat.

'Now try this.' Madge poured a small amount from the second teapot. Kevin grabbed an extra cup from the display.

Baz accepted it and looked at her friends. 'I'm not sure what you're getting me into here.' She sniffed the contents before taking a sip. 'Ooh, that is lovely. I think I'll have that one, please.'

As Madge poured, Kevin explained. 'That's the Pornstar Nan. It's based on the Martini. Now, what did you ladies want to chat about?'

Madge poured and distributed drinks while Peggy spoke. 'Our friend's granddaughter was here a few weeks ago and while she was here, she met a young man. This man was very charming and what have you ... but he's been cruelly using this poor young woman ever since. We're trying to track him down. And also to see if you've heard of similar happening to anyone else.'

Kevin pulled over another chair. 'I'll be happy to help if I can. Can't have people preying on our community.'

Still pouring the final cocktail, Madge wagged her left index finger in Kevin's direction. 'Exactly what I said. Didn't I say that?'

'Now, what's this fellow's name and what does he look like? I have a sneaky feeling I know who you mean but let's see if the details match up.'

Baz pulled out her phone and started tapping away. 'His name is Tom Porter – or at least that's the name he gave Daisy. And this' – she held the phone up for Kevin to see – 'is the nearest she could get to a photo.'

Peggy peered across the table. 'Pass that around, would you? We might recognise him.'

Kevin took the phone from Baz and zoomed in on the image. He chuckled. 'I doubt anyone's going to recognise anything from this. No offence, Ms Spencer – Baz.'

Kevin passed the phone to Madge, who pulled her glasses up to her eyes and squinted. 'Can't tell anything.' She passed the phone to Peggy.

The image on screen showed Daisy and a blurry figure beside her. He could have been white, Asian, or mixed race. Probably anywhere from eighteen to thirty-five. The only thing she could see from the image was that he was a bit taller than Daisy. He'd have to be somewhere in the six-foot range – 183 centimetres in new money.

Peggy passed the phone to Carole. 'Hand that back to Baz, would you, love?'

Carole glanced at the phone as she did so. 'That's Tom Jackson, that is.'

Everyone stared at Carole. People often assumed that her bizarre and sometimes incomprehensible contributions to conversations meant she wasn't paying attention. But after all these years, Peggy knew better.

Still, it came as a bit of a shock that anyone could make such a definitive ID from that blurry image. 'What makes you so sure, love?'

'Tattoo of a cross on his neck.' Carole picked up her teacup and downed half of the contents in one go. 'Remember how angry his nan was when he got that?'

Madge chuckled. 'Indeed I do. She tanned his fifteen-year-old hide.'

'Give me that!' Peggy grabbed the phone from Carole's hand and squinted at it. 'Well, I'll be...' She looked at Baz. 'I think she's right.'

Kevin got up and stood behind Peggy, peering over her shoulder. 'Yeah, that's what I feared.'

'Quit reading over my shoulder.' Peggy swatted the impertinent lad away. She passed the phone back to Baz.

'Sorry, Ms Trent.' Kevin returned to his seat.

'Now, explain what you meant.' Madge topped everyone's drinks up.

'Tom lives in my building, so I hear stuff. After his nan died, he did some time in Thameside. You know – the prison? After he got out, I heard rumours he started scamming people. He'd find a mark, pretend to be interested in them. He didn't discriminate by gender or age or whatever – the only common thread seemed to be that they were the sorts of people who would give you the shirt off their back.' Kevin put his hand to his mouth. 'That's not what he did to your granddaughter, is it?'

Baz balanced her cup and saucer on her knee. 'Sounds like it, yes.'

'Oh, gosh. I'm so sorry.' Kevin laid a hand on Baz's arm. 'What a dreadful man. I've seen him come in here a couple of times – but I always make him leave. If they met here, it must have happened on a night I wasn't working.'

Baz smiled. 'Thank you, Kevin. Can you elaborate on what you've heard? What's his MO? Any victims who might be willing to have a chat with us?'

'So...' Kevin crossed his legs and leant in. 'From what I've heard, he preys on people's vulnerabilities. Tells them he needs money to pay rent, child support, to invest in new business endeavours, to buy clothes for a job interview – know what I mean? In one case, I heard he even told a guy he needed money to start up a porn studio. He's got a million stories.'

'How long has this rapscallion been running these cons?' Peggy couldn't believe the community had just been letting this man get away with this. Well, she *could* believe it; she just didn't want to.

'I think he got out of prison a few months back ... so probably about that long.' Kevin shrugged. 'What can I say? He's very charming. People want to believe the best.'

Madge sucked air through her teeth. 'Disgraceful.'

Baz picked a cake up from the platter and placed it on her plate. 'Tell me, does he even have kids? Or an ex-wife?'

Kevin put a hand to his heart. 'Oh my days. Can you imagine? No, thank heavens. What a terrible father he'd be! I don't think he has any family left.'

Baz nodded.

'Anyway, I don't know anyone who's fallen for his schemes, but I think I might know someone who knows someone. If you leave me your number, I'll see if I can't pass it along.'

Kevin stood up. 'It's hard to believe we have two predators running around the neighbourhood at the same time. You've heard about the ... the assaults, haven't you?'

'We have indeed,' Peggy replied.

Madge pointed at the chair Kevin had just abandoned. 'Sit back down, young man.'

'What do you know about them?' Baz asked.

'Well.' Kevin resumed his seat as instructed. 'I've heard about a few incidents around the area. Always young women. Whoever this guy is, he waits at bus stops then follows them as they get off the bus and then he—' Kevin looked at the company he was in. 'Well, he does stuff to them. Right out in public.'

Peggy pressed her fingers to her temples. 'The word is rape, Kevin. We won't swoon just because you call it what it is.' She pulled out a calling card with her name and contact details on it and passed it over to the bartender.

Kevin sighed as he accepted the card. 'I know – I just don't like to think about it. It's awful.' He stood up. 'I'll pass your number on to my friend for him to give to his cousin. If she wants to talk to you, she'll ring. I really should be getting back to work.' He stood and tucked the card into his trouser pocket.

'Thank you for your time, Kevin.' Baz smiled at the young man.

———

LATER THAT EVENING when she was just washing up after dinner, Peggy received a voicemail from a withheld number.

'Hiya. I heard you was wanting to know about Tom and that scam he's doing – know what I mean? He got 400 quid offa me afore I figured him out. Told me his kids needed money for food. And then later he said he needed money to pay his tuition 'cause he'd be kicked out of college. I don't want to meet you – I just want to get on wiv my life but I thought maybe my story would help – know what I mean?'

Peggy took a deep breath. She opened the group chat she shared with the girls and told them about the message.

Carole's phone buzzed on the shelf next to her but she didn't so much as glance at it.

Peggy sat down next to her on the sofa. 'We found another victim. Of the swindler, I mean. Not the sexual predator.' She put her arm around her partner and snuggled into her. 'Though, I suppose this is another type of sexual predator.'

Carole leant over and kissed her softly. 'Take away their growth hormone and they'd all be classified as children.' She turned her attention back to the telly.

Peggy held her hand. When her phone buzzed, she used her free hand to pull it out of her pocket.

MADGE

We need to act.

BAZ

With a second victim, we should go to the police.

Peggy scoffed and tapped out a reply.

PEGGY

Well, I suppose we could try.

BAZ

What else are we going to do?

MADGE

We confront him!

BAZ

And then what?

MADGE

...

The elusive ellipsis that indicated Madge was typing remained in place for a while but no text was ever sent. Peggy pictured Madge sitting in her flat, typing and deleting sentences over and over.

PEGGY

Well, no time like the present. Shall we go now?

———

HALF AN HOUR LATER, Baz pulled up in a cab. At least the rain had stopped. Peggy climbed in and fastened her seatbelt. The driver dropped them at Lewisham nick a few minutes after that.

Before they'd even entered the building, the front door slid open and two figures walked out.

Peter smiled – but it looked like a smile of confusion rather than one of welcome. Not unfriendly just ... perplexed. 'Ms Trent. Ms Spencer. What are you doing here?'

Mike elbowed Peter in the side and flashed his dimply grin

at the women. 'Way to make them feel welcome. How can we help you, ladies?'

Putting weight on her cane, Peggy pulled herself up to her full height. 'We are here to report a crime.'

'Well,' said Baz. 'We just wanted to have a little chat about a local man who's been making a nuisance of himself.'

Both men's faces fell.

'Oh my days.' Peter took a step towards Peggy. 'Did someone hurt you, Auntie?'

Scowling, Peggy waved the young man away. 'Nothing like that.'

Baz explained in brief about Tom Jackson's activities, using police lingo. She managed to sum it all up in just a few words.

'Since neither of you is the victim, there's not a huge amount we can do.' Mike put a reassuring hand on Baz's arm, making her flush. 'But I'll tell you what. We're just finishing our shifts for the evening. But if you give us this bloke's name and details, we'll arrange to go round and have a little chat with him tomorrow. Would that suit you?'

Peggy scowled. 'It seems like a cop-out.' And, yes, the pun was fully intended.

The officer nodded. 'I do understand, Ms Trent. But the thing is, we'd need to hear from the victims themselves.'

Peggy pulled herself up to her full height. 'You're not even going to take a police report?'

Peter looked uncomfortable but Mike flashed a dimply smile, which seemed to leave Baz swooning. 'We'll have a chat with him tomorrow. If we don't like what we hear and if you can persuade one of the actual victims to come forwards, then there may be a case to answer for.' He held up an index finger. '*If.*'

'Thank you, Officers,' said Baz.

CHAPTER 7

wherein ill behaviour abounds

BAZ AND DAISY had a quiet Sunday. They went to the local Tesco for some shopping and then Baz spent the afternoon perfecting her Bakewell tartlet recipe. Daisy made them some dinner and they sat together, drinking wine and watching a hospital drama on Netflix. Before they knew it, it was time to get ready for bed.

Baz had a shower and changed into her nightgown. When she emerged from the en suite, she could hear voices from the hallway. Had Daisy put the TV back on?

But no. That was Daisy's voice. Baz crept to the bedroom door and listened. She could hear a man as well.

Throwing her dressing gown on, she crept to the hall to see what was happening. She tied the sash as she peered round the corner. Daisy was at the door with a man. From what Baz could see, it appeared he was trying to argue his way into the flat.

They hadn't noticed her, so she dialled 999.

'Police, fire, or ambulance?'

'Police, please,' she whispered.

'I'm sorry,' said the operator. 'I'm going to need you to speak up.'

With a groan, Baz returned to the en suite. She didn't like leaving Daisy alone with that man, but she also wanted help. 'Police, please,' she said more clearly.

She waited while they transferred her call, every second feeling like an hour. Daisy's voice still carried from the hall.

'Police. What's your emergency?'

'Hi, yes. Someone's trying to break into my flat.'

Baz could hear the young woman on the other end of the line typing as she spoke. 'When you say he's trying to get in, what exactly do you mean? Are you home or are you observing this from elsewhere?'

Baz's stomach felt like a rock. 'I'm inside the flat.'

'Are you alone?'

'Yes. I mean, no.' She'd always wondered why innocent people sometimes sounded so muddled when reporting a crime. 'My granddaughter's here.'

'How old is your granddaughter?'

'Nineteen.'

Baz heard the clicking of keys as the operator took down the info. 'Okay, and can you tell me exactly what's happening, please?'

'Daisy – that's my granddaughter – she's at the door with him. He's trying to bully his way in.'

There was a pause and the sound of typing before the operator spoke again. 'Okay, can I ask, does she know the man?'

'I think it's her ex-boyfriend.' Baz clutched her dressing gown to her throat.

'All right, ma'am. The police are on their way.'

Baz felt the rock in her stomach dissipate. 'Thank God. Can you give me an indication of how long they'll be, please?'

'They've got a few calls ahead of you, so it will probably be an hour or two.'

A chill ran through Baz. 'Two hours?'

'That's correct.'

With a frustrated sigh, Baz shook her head. 'Tell them not to bother. I'll deal with him myself. I'll call back if we still need you.' She stabbed the screen with her finger to disconnect the call.

She dropped the phone onto the vanity but then picked it up and dialled the concierge instead, cursing herself for not calling them in the first place.

'Reception. How can I help?' Not Jessica's voice. An Irish voice. James, Baz thought his name was. She tried to picture him in her mind.

'This is Barbara Spencer from unit 907. I've got an aggressive young man trying to bully my granddaughter into letting him into my flat. Would you please tell me how in the f— fudge this man got past you?'

'I'll be right there.'

'Thank you.' Baz disconnected again. This time she dropped the phone into her pocket.

She headed out into the hall once more, this time approaching the arguing pair.

Tom was about the same height as Daisy, maybe an inch or two taller. But he was throwing himself around as if he wanted her to know he could hurt her if he wanted to – he *could* but he wouldn't.

Baz had seen that sort of behaviour often enough in her career. Hint to a person that you had the power to harm them – then tell them bluntly you never would. It made the victim believe the problem existed only in their own mind.

Tom was all wounded charm. 'How could you do this to me,

Daisy? I'm my kids' sole breadwinner. If I go to prison, who'll look after them?'

He carried on like that as Baz approached. She could see Daisy beginning to cave – she was actually falling for this flim-flam. 'Sorry, Nan. We didn't mean to wake you. Tom and I were ... we were just talking.'

Daisy looked like she might invite him in, so Baz put herself between him and Daisy. 'You're not welcome here.'

Tom smiled. 'Come on. We're just talking. No harm.' He raised his hands in self-defence.

'No.' Baz crossed her arms over her chest. 'You've done enough damage already.'

Daisy put her hand on Baz's arm. 'It's okay, Nan. It's fine. Really.'

'No, it isn't.' Baz refused to budge.

A cold fury in the way Tom looked at her sent a chill down her spine. He looked past her at Daisy. 'How could you do this to me? You think if this ever went to court anyone would believe a—'

Behind him there was a ding as the lift doors opened. Baz's heart raced – her mind was awhirl.

'Everything all right, ma'am?' Baz couldn't see the concierge's face through Tom's bulk but she could see his shoes.

Tom raised his hands and flashed a cheerful grin as he spun around. 'No worries. Ain't nuffink happening. Just a friendly chat. If Daisy tells me to go, I'll go.'

It looked like Daisy was wavering but after several heart-beats, she nodded. 'I think it's for the best.'

Tom spun back to face her. Once again, he used his bulk to his advantage. 'What's that, love? I didn't quite catch it.'

Baz swallowed. 'She said you should go.'

Tom smiled at Baz, but it had ice in it. 'I ain't talking to you. This don't concern you. It's between me and Daisy – mind your business.'

His words had the opposite effect he seemed to intend. Daisy exhaled. 'I want you to leave. Please.'

'You heard the lady,' said James. 'Come with me, big fella. I remember you now. You snuck in with the couple from the fifth floor. Made it look like you were with them.'

'Dunno what you're talking about, mate.' On his way past, Tom leant close to Baz and whispered, 'No bother. Someone else will be *grateful* for my affection.' He winked so that only she could see it – as though the two of them had just shared a cheeky little joke.

Baz looked at Daisy, but she didn't seem to have noticed anything had passed between Tom and Baz.

Tom headed towards the lift. 'Anything else you ladies need?' asked James.

Baz put a hand to her chest. 'Thank you. I think we're all right now.'

Daisy nodded.

'If you're sure.' James joined Tom at the lift. 'Just ring the front desk if you need anything else.'

Daisy headed for the kitchen as the lift arrived and the two men got in. As the doors slid shut, Tom smiled once again and waved at Baz. It sent a shiver down her spine.

Her heart racing, Baz followed Daisy. 'I was all ready to get into bed but now my adrenaline's pumping and I doubt I'll be able to sleep.'

'Don't worry about it,' said Daisy. 'He was just feeling bad about how we left things. He came here to apologise.'

Baz's breath caught. 'What?'

Picking the kettle up off its stand, Daisy faced Baz. 'Sorry, do you want?'

Baz nodded.

Daisy filled the kettle, then set it back in place, and flicked it on. 'Anyways, yeah. He wanted to talk about what happened.' She leant back against the counter. 'I'm kinda conflicted, actually. I mean, on the one hand, it was sweet of him to come and apologise. On the other hand, I would've preferred a text. You know?'

Baz gritted her teeth. 'You can't be serious! There was nothing sweet about his presence here tonight.'

Daisy shook her head. 'It was! He even offered to pay back the money I loaned him. Just to show me how serious he was.'

Classic emotional manipulation tactic. 'This' – Baz waved a hand towards the door where the encounter had so recently ended – 'was not an apology. It was about control, pure and simple. You do not show up at someone's home in the middle of the night unannounced to apologise. Sneaking past security isn't an apology.'

Daisy crossed her arms over her chest. 'You just can't handle someone else being close to me. You want me all to yourself – but it isn't going to be that way forever.'

Baz pinched the bridge of her nose and breathed slowly. 'Daisy, no. It's just... Trust me, I know a manipulator when I see one.'

Daisy stomped her feet and let out a formless yell of frustration. 'Your old job has warped your mind and you can't even see it. You think everyone is out to get everyone else all the time. Especially me. You think I'm this poor innocent child and the whole world wants to hurt me. Everywhere you look, you see crooks and villains. It's not healthy.'

Baz clutched her chest. 'Th... No... It's...' She closed her fist and pressed it to her lips, buying time to compose her thoughts. 'That's not what this is, I promise. He told me if you didn't take him back he'd find someone else to scam.'

Daisy took a step away and raised her hands in a blocking

motion. 'That didn't happen. You know I was there, right? If he'd said that, I'd have heard him. Gah! You're unbelievable.'

Baz gripped the counter to keep herself upright. 'You're absolutely correct that I want to protect you. Of course I do, but that's not wha—'

Daisy waved dismissively. 'Just forget it. I'm going to bed.' She stomped out of the room. A few seconds later, the flat shook with the slamming of her door.

Baz looked at the clock on the microwave – half past eleven. She went to bed; she wouldn't sleep but she didn't know what else to do.

———

'The thing that I love most,' Sam said to John as they strolled through the beautiful garden at Sayes Court, 'is music. Then maybe you.'

It seemed like no bad thing. To be Sam's second favourite thing. 'What's the point of being there then?'

Sam touched his hand to John's chest. 'Why the point is me and you and what we want to happen ... amongst other things, of course.' He smiled endearingly.

John laughed at the answer, adjusting his already perfect sleeves. 'Let's not make jest of ourselves, Sam. You don't have to find excuses. A man as fine as yourself should know that already.'

'Oh, my dearest Evie.'

PEGGY STOPPED TYPING and studied what she'd written. While it was hardly the sort of thing she wanted to read, she had to admit the readers liked it. She wouldn't get rich off her fiction –

but it did bring in a nice bit of cash every month. She looked at the time: just about midnight.

'Suppose we'd better tidy up.' She pulled herself to her feet. Carole joined her in the kitchen. As always, Carole washed and Peggy dried. Peggy put the dishes away as soon as she'd towelled them off. They'd tried switching tasks a few times over the years – just to break up the monotony. But each time, Peggy'd had to spend ages searching for the dishes.

Drinking glasses in the oven. Dinner plates atop the fridge-freezer. She'd even found a set of cutlery in a cupboard in the block's communal hall once.

When they finished, Carole set to wiping down the sides as Peggy emptied the rubbish. Cookie eagerly followed her to the front door. 'It's not time for walkies yet, mister. Soon, I promise. You can come with me to the bins – but no further.'

Peggy tied the rubbish bag and hooked it over her cane, with Cookie's nose pressing at the back of her knees right behind her. She swore at the block's troublesome front door as she struggled to open it.

The moment the door gave way, Cookie pushed past her and ran out into the block's front court, barking like a bastard. Peggy dropped her bag on the lobby floor.

'You get back here right this—' But before Peggy could finish that sentence, Cookie barked at a figure in the courtyard. She was standing in the bright light of the doorway, looking out at the dark, making it hard for her to make sense of what she was seeing. The man appeared to drop a rubbish bag he'd been holding in front of himself. Thus unburdened, he scarpered, the gate clattering behind him.

Peggy shook her head as she followed Cookie into the garden. 'That's right,' she called to the departed figure. 'You run off. I'll clean up after you.' She walked towards the mess the man had left, muttering as she moved. 'Bloody fly-tippers.'

She stopped dead in her tracks as her eyes finally began adjusting to the darkness.

Cookie squatted low and licked the crumpled heap on the ground. It wasn't a bag of rubbish the man had dropped – it was a person.

Peggy tried to shoo the dog away but he wouldn't leave the person alone.

The girl flung her arms around Cookie's neck and sobbed into his shoulder.

Peggy squinted and tried to get a good look at her. 'Are you okay?' Immediately, she chided herself for her stupidity. Of course she wasn't okay.

'Come on, let's get you inside.' Peggy held her right arm out for the girl – hoping the cane in her left hand could take the extra weight.

The girl released Cookie and hauled herself to her feet, still crying. Once she was upright, she threw her arms around Peggy instead. A wet face pressed into Peggy's neck. She steered them both into the lobby. Fortunately, the front door had wedged itself open, so Peggy only had to give it a good shove with her shoulder.

It was only once they were standing in the washed-out light of the building's foyer that Peggy realised who it was she held in her arms. Emmy, her lovely, young upstairs neighbour.

Peggy pulled herself away so she could get a better look. 'What happened?' She didn't really need to ask, though. Emmy's coat was half off, her shirt was torn, and her skirt was all rumpled. 'Doesn't matter. I'll call the ambulance.' She didn't have her phone on her, though – she'd have to get it from the flat.

Peggy raised her hand to her face and fought down the bile. She'd been in the living room – only a few metres away while this sweet girl was attacked. If she'd come out five minutes earlier, she'd have ripped the man apart with her bare hands.

Peggy looked at her free hand. Not these hands. These hands were long past the days when they could perform such visceral acts. She cursed her decrepit body.

No, she wouldn't let herself get caught up in self-recriminations. 'Let's just go into my place for a sec, so I can get my phone to call the ambulance.' She tried to steer the girl towards her door – just a few steps from where they stood.

'No!' Emmy shrieked and pulled away from her, beginning to tumble back to the floor.

Peggy struggled to maintain her grip on the girl. 'You really should get checked out, my dear.' She wasn't sure what she'd do if Emmy passed out on the floor.

'No. Just let me sleep.' The girl collapsed back into her. 'Tomorrow, I promise. First thing in the morning. Just ... not now.'

With a sigh, Peggy conceded. She directed her towards the stairs. Wrapping her arm around Emmy's waist, she guided her up the stairs. Fortunately, the poor thing was mostly carrying her own weight. Mostly. Cookie stayed right behind them – if Peggy failed to get the girl and herself up the stairs, he'd be the one to pay the price.

They made it up without incident, though. When they got to Emmy's door, Peggy asked her if she had her keys handy.

The girl's hand was shaking badly as she tried to dig through her handbag.

Peggy held a hand out. 'May I?'

Emmy shoved the bag into Peggy's hands and let out another sob. Oh great, she had one of those key rings. There had to be at least two dozen keys. *Why do people need so many keys?* Peggy picked a key at random and put it into the lock.

She'd unsuccessfully tried four keys when she heard the

door being unbolted from the inside. Well, thank heavens for that.

Amrita, Emmy's flatmate, pulled the door open. 'Lemme guess, you've had a bit too much to drink and can't remember which—' When she spied the scene at her door, she flung it all the way open and got out of the way so Peggy could lead Emmy in. 'Oh my days. What happened?'

'She was attacked. I found her out front. Cookie chased off the bastard who did it.'

It was the same layout as Peggy's flat. She didn't know which bedroom was Emmy's but she knew where to find the living room. Having steered the girl to the sofa, she handed her off to her friend. 'I'll put the kettle on.'

Amrita lowered Emmy to a sitting position as Peggy fumbled in the almost-but-not-quite-familiar kitchen. She made as little noise as she could while she filled the kettle and found a couple of clean mugs in the cupboard. She fished teabags out of the pack. All the while, she kept an eye on the two girls in the living room. Cookie wouldn't leave Emmy's side.

While she waited for the kettle to boil, she approached the girls. 'Shall I ring the paramedics now?'

'No!' Emmy shouted. She sniffed. 'No, I mean. Thank you. You've been so nice. I will do something about it. Just not right now. I can't deal with anything more tonight. Please.' She was overcome by wracking sobs once again. Amrita pulled her close and stroked her hair.

Peggy went back to the kitchen and poured water into two mugs. Sugar was out of fashion; she doubted either woman took it in their tea. She opened the fridge. No milk but there was a carton of almond milk in the door. She gave it a sniff and then poured a splash into both mugs.

Carrying the tea through to the living room, she looked around. It was vibrant but neat – full of a mix of Argos value range furniture and well-used pieces that looked like they'd once been high end. The walls were bedecked with large original paintings that looked like they were all the work of one artist.

Peggy set the two mugs on the table, then used her chin to beckon Amrita into the hall with her. Emmy cried, 'Please don't leave me alone.' Poor Emmy. She looked so small. So very small.

Amrita shushed her and stroked her hair. 'It's okay. I promise I'll be right back. I just need to talk to Peggy for a minute.'

Emmy bit her lip and then nodded. 'Okay.' She sniffed again.

Leaving Emmy to Cookie's care, Amrita followed Peggy into the hall. 'Was she raped?'

Peggy nodded once. 'I think so. But I'm not sure. There's a sexual health clinic over at Waldron – by New Cross station. You should take her there first thing tomorrow. Maybe the police too – if she's willing.' She studied the worn beige carpet. 'Don't let her bathe first. They'll need to do ... tests.'

Tears flowed down Amrita's brown face. She brushed them away with the back of her hand. 'I will. Thank you. I should get back to her. You can come and check on her in the morning if you want.' She pulled the door open for Peggy.

Peggy touched Emmy's shoulder awkwardly. 'I will. Thank you for looking after her.' She raised her chin but not her voice. 'Cookie, it's time to go home.'

CHAPTER 8

in which tales are told

WHEN BAZ WALKED into the kitchen, Daisy was pouring herself a glass of juice. 'I'm so sorry, Nan.' She set the carton down, then ran and threw her arms around Baz. 'I was upset last night – but I know better. If you said that's what you heard, then that's what he said. I should have believed you.'

'Oh, Daisy.' A night of tossing and turning in bed had left Baz feeling vulnerable and she burst into tears. She'd not had a fight with Daisy in ages. Not really. Not a proper one. 'It made me miserable, thinking you were angry at me.'

Daisy pulled back, away from her grandmother, but clung to her hands. 'I *was* angry. Only partially at you – not because I believed you were wrong. I was mad because you made me confront the truth. I fell for a conman. I shouldn't have but I did. So I was pissed off at you, at him ... but mainly at me. How could I have been so naïve?'

Baz cupped Daisy's face in her hands. 'You have a good heart. Instinct tells you to believe the best in people.' She released her granddaughter and began rummaging through the cupboards. 'On the one hand, I don't ever want that to change about you. You're a beautiful soul. But on the other...' She slammed the third cupboard in a row. 'I'm sorry, I've got a pounding headache and a craving for comfort food. What say we go to Jenny's for breakfast?'

Daisy sagged against the counter. 'Oh my gosh, yes. I've been standing here staring at food, trying to figure out what I want. Let me just grab my backpack. I'll be ready to go in a minute.'

Baz removed a light cotton jacket and her handbag from the hall cupboard. Once she'd put her shoes on, she dropped the keys into her bag and patted herself down. 'Keys, phone, purse. Embroidery's already in the mobility scooter's basket. I think I'm good to go.'

Daisy was just sliding her left foot into a ridiculously impractical flat. There was no way it provided any support or even cushioning. *Oh to be young and not have to worry about such things.*

A few minutes later, Baz steered the scooter out the tower block's door. Ahead of them, Deptford Bridge station was filling up with commuters on their way into Canary Wharf. They turned left and then left again onto Deptford Broadway, which became New Cross Road once they crossed Brookmill Road. Jenny's was a greasy spoon. And it had the benefit of being almost directly across from Wellbeloved.

Baz had visited the caff several times over the past few months. She didn't think Jenny was a real person. For all Baz knew, she never had been. The two women walked in the door. A young man smiled and told them to go ahead and sit anywhere they liked.

They picked a seat by the window. The young man took their order and then scuttled off.

Baz looked out at the road. A double-decker red bus was

stopped at the light. After it drove off, she could still barely see Wellbeloved's cheerful yellow awning through the fog.

———

TWENTY MINUTES LATER, Baz paid up. Daisy hugged her before heading for the bus stop. Baz waited for the light to change and then steered her scooter over the road to Wellbeloved.

The others were already in their usual places with their beverages mostly – or, in Peggy's case, entirely – finished before Baz arrived. The cosy warmth and the delicious scents of the café lifted her heart.

Slinging her bag down by her seat, Baz smiled at her friends. 'Morning, ladies. Just going to go place my order. Anyone need a top-up?'

'Good of you to join us.' Madge paused her knitting and turned to face Baz. 'I'm good. Thank you.'

Cookie stood up and made like he was ready to leave. Peggy shook her head dismissively. 'Not now, you ninny.' She snapped her fingers and he sat back down. Turning to Baz, she added, 'What kept you this morning? Sleep in?'

Baz reached out to give Cookie a quick pat. 'Sorry, something interesting happened last night. Let me order my tea and I'll tell you everything.'

'Tell Sarah I'll have another espresso when she's got a moment.' Peggy clicked a few keys on her laptop.

'Honestly, Peggy,' Baz replied. 'At your age, I don't know how you can take so much caffeine. At any age, frankly.'

Peggy half chuckled, half scowled as she cocked her head. 'Haven't you figured out my dirty little secret yet?'

Baz paused. 'I'm sorry?'

'My dear, it's decaf. It's always decaf.'

Baz considered that. 'What – even the first one of the day?'

Peggy waggled her eyebrows suggestively. '*Especially* the first one of the day.'

Baz blinked. 'Okay. Won't be two ticks.' A few minutes later, after placing the orders, she returned.

Peggy looked up. 'So?'

Taking her usual seat, Baz began, 'I had a little spat with Daisy last night. This morning we went for a nice breakfast and talked it all through.'

Baz pulled her embroidery from her bag and set to work as she filled her friends in on her evening's adventures. 'Anyways, it was lucky the concierge came along when he did. I don't know what I'd have done if Daisy had actually let him in.'

'Times like that are when a good knitting needle comes in handy.' Carole jabbed the air with a disturbingly sharp-looking metal implement. 'Amateurs always think you're best to go in through the eye but that's a myth. Unless you have exceptionally good aim and a co-operative victim, you're just going to bounce off—'

'Carole, dear.' Peggy smiled awkwardly as she touched her on the knee. 'I don't think that's what Baz had in mind.'

'Good.' Returning her focus to her knitting, Carole nodded. 'Into the ear is best. A delicate manoeuvre, sure. But effective if you get it right.'

Baz shook her head. 'Yes, well, I didn't do either of those things. Though part of me wishes I had.' She slapped a hand to her mouth, surprised by the violence of her own mind. Between the cold brutality of Carole's suggestion and the reality of Tom's words the night before, Baz began to shake. She kept inadvertently stabbing her fingers with the fine embroidery needle in her hands. If she'd had a weapon to hand – even a knitting needle – she might have done as Carole suggested.

'Maybe I ought to take up knitting instead.' Baz held up her left hand, revealing the droplets of blood flowing from her index and middle fingers. Madge passed her a serviette.

'Good for the soul,' said Carole brightly.

'Mmm hmm,' added Madge. Baz hoped they were both referring to knitting rather than violence.

Just then, Sarah arrived with the drinks order. 'Sorry it's taken so long, ladies. Bit of a mad rush this morning.'

Baz smiled at her. 'Thank you.' Sarah returned to the main room. 'It's just... I don't ever want Daisy to become so jaded with the world that she loses that optimism – that ability to see the good in everyone around her.'

Peggy arched an eyebrow. 'That naïveté?'

'Well, yes. Okay, there is that.' Baz grinned. She took a sip of her tea. 'I suppose it is naïveté of a sort. But it's more than that. It's her kind-hearted nature. She's grown into a strong, smart, beautiful woman – all of which is great. But her generosity of spirit is her best feature.' She exhaled slowly. 'Anyways, by the time I finally got to bed it was midnight. And I don't think I fell asleep until almost three.'

'It's interesting,' Peggy said. 'As I mentioned earlier, you were not the only one who had an interesting late-night adventure.'

'Oh, yes. I forgot. What did you get up to?' Baz leant forwards and poured herself some tea.

As Peggy revealed what had happened the night before, Baz struggled to contain her horror. Her stomach churned as she listened to Peggy's tale of the girl she'd encountered in the forecourt.

'I'm so sorry. That's awful. And I feel terribly for that young lass.' Baz frowned. 'What about a hospital? They really should examine her – do a rape kit. They'll need to run the DNA – check for matches.'

'She wouldn't go anywhere last night.' Peggy squeezed the arm of her chair so hard, Baz feared she might leave a mark. Sometimes victims – and that included witnesses – could be quite visceral in their reactions. 'The flatmate, Amrita, said she'd spend the night with her so she didn't have to be alone.'

Baz rubbed her jaw. 'So no DNA.' So much for that idea.

Peggy's lips twisted. 'Amrita promised me she'd get Emmy over to the health centre as soon as they woke up.'

'Waldron's just down the way.' Madge used her knitting needle to gesture westwards. 'They do testing and provide counselling.'

'Okay,' Baz said. 'So maybe she will make a report. Hopefully.' Well, that was something, at least.

Baz looked from one of her friends to the next. 'My gosh. That poor girl.' She clenched her jaw for a moment as she considered her next words. 'I spent many years having to deal with ... unpleasant events. Professionally, I mean. And even still, hearing about such matters leaves me feeling broken and empty.' She faced Peggy with a shake of her head. 'How are you still functioning this morning? Why aren't you a complete wreck?'

Peggy and Madge exchanged one of those meaningful glances.

'I forget sometimes that you weren't always a woman,' Madge said then pinched her lips shut. 'No, I mean. That was rude – I'm sorry. But I'm not sure what the appropriate phrasing is.'

Baz narrowed her eyes. 'I know what you mean – but at the same time I don't. That is, you're correct that I didn't always live openly and authentically as my true self. But I'm not sure what that has to do with this situation.'

Peggy pulled her mouth into a tight pucker. 'What Madge is so inarticulately trying to say is that women deal with these matters. Women have *always* dealt with such things. We do it because we have to. We do it because sometimes ... the law isn't on our side. And even when it is, it may not be enforced in a way that's helpful. And if we fell apart every time we heard of another woman being harmed — whether that harm is physical or emotional, sexual or not — well, then nothing would ever get resolved. So we carry on living, loving, and laughing because we must. And to honour the memory of those who have gone before — those who have fought to make our lives easier ... bit by bit.'

Baz breathed out slowly. 'I'm sorry.'

Peggy shrugged. 'Why are you sorry? You didn't attack that girl. To the best of my knowledge, you never attacked anyone. This isn't your fault.'

Taking a moment to pull herself together, Baz closed her eyes. 'Well, it sounds like you made that young woman's experience a bit less awful than it would otherwise have been.' She forced herself to smile. 'And, Peggy, it sounds like you earned a full-caf shot this morning.'

Peggy chuckled. 'Gives me wind.'

They sat in silence for a few minutes. Only the soft sound of Peggy's keyboard, Madge and Carole's knitting needles, and Cookie scratching his ear pierced the hush.

Sarah came through into the room and collected used dishes and detritus from the other tables, piling everything neatly onto a tray. But then instead of heading back to the other side of the shop, she dragged over a chair and sat down next to her mother, the loaded tray on her lap.

Madge leant forwards and studied her daughter. 'What is it?'

Sarah sighed. 'Look, I'm not sure if I should tell you this. I don't want you to go all Jessica Fletcher on the case.'

Peggy took her fingers off her keyboard and looked up.

'Well, okay,' Sarah began. 'I know you ladies are investigating the Goldsmiths Groper.'

The women all looked at each other. Well, except Carole, of course, who looked at nothing in particular.

'I'm sorry, what euphemistic nonsense is this?' Peggy's eyes narrowed.

'Oh. That's what I was referring to. There's an article this morning.' Sarah waved at Peggy's computer. 'Pull up the BBC News and go to the London local page.'

The four women watched Peggy as she clicked a few keys. 'Ah.' She turned the computer around to face the others.

Madge pulled her glasses down her nose and squinted at the images and corresponding text on screen. 'I can't read that. What's it say?'

Peggy turned the device back to face herself and read aloud. '"Goldsmiths Groper strikes again" – what a load of old tosh! The man's a rapist. Trust me – I've seen his handiwork. Calling him a *groper* is pure toxic masculinity. It's nothing but a way of trivialising his offences – making him sound like a naughty schoolboy going around fondling or tickling people.'

Madge waved an impatient hand at Peggy. 'We know all that. Just read the article.' Out the corner of her eye, Baz noticed Sarah bite her lip.

Peggy scowled at her screen. '"Anyone with more information, please ring our newsroom on" blah blah blah. There's a photo of that bizarre sculpture atop the main Goldsmiths building. Here we go, "Local residents report a disturbing number of sexual assaults across Deptford and New Cross in the borough of Lewisham in south-east London. The incidents are believed to have happened over the past four months. The perpetrator appears to favour young women, many of who are —" Now that is appalling. Many of *who* indeed. Does no one edit this rag?'

'Oh, just skip over the grammatical errors – for goodness sake.' Madge shook her head. 'We'll take them as read.'

Peggy tsked but carried on reading. '"Many of *whom* are believed to be students. It is believed he follows them as they get off the bus. Most of the attacks have taken place in public. One victim, who spoke to this reporter on condition of anonymity, said she had been sexually assaulted in her own front garden. Her flatmates were horrified to discover their friend had been—" Oh, for pity's sake! The lengths people will go to to avoid the word rape – as if it's the word rather than the fact that is somehow offensive.'

Sarah was nodding in agreement but at a look from Madge, Peggy carried on reading crossly. 'Blah blah euphemism blah. Ooh hoo! You'll love this bit, Madge. "Local resident, Clive Chen says the—"'

Peggy's voice was drowned out by Madge's scornful laughter at that point. 'My gosh! That man is so full of himself. He just cannot keep his beak out of things. Imagine taking it upon yourself to speak on behalf of a community you're barely even a part of. You know, I bet he's the rapist.'

'Mum!' Sarah raised a hand. 'You can't go accusing people of something like that just because you don't like them. Now can you let Auntie finish reading the article, please?'

Madge waved her daughter away. 'Fine, fine.'

'Whatever. Madge, it won't shock you to learn Clive said nothing useful or even interesting. Man just likes to hear himself talk. Anyhoo... Blah blah... Oh! Here's something we didn't know. "The two common features all the victims appear to agreed on"' – Peggy let out a long sigh at the obvious error – '"is that the man sounded local and had a very charming manner." More poorly edited blah blah blah. Aha, now this bit is interesting – though not surprising, I suppose. The last line of the article says, "Metropolitan Police did not respond to our requests for comment on this story.'"

Carole released a string of profanity that would have made a sailor blush. Peggy scowled.

'They know.' Baz felt her spirit fall. 'The police know there's a serial predator on the loose.'

'But do they care about the women of this community?' Madge sucked her teeth. 'They do not.'

Peggy shook her head. 'Of course not. This is Lewisham. Look at the demographics of this area. We have students and we have working-class people and we have immigrants. Almost half of the people here are non-white. A third of our population live in poverty. The Battle of Lewisham. The New Cross House Fire. The Met would care if this happened in Surrey or Chelsea. But not Lewisham. To them, we are disposable.'

Madge waved a hand in a flippant, dismissive sort of gesture. 'A few minutes ago you were lecturing us on how we can't resolve anything if we fall apart. So tell me... How will this rant fix anything?'

Peggy fixed Madge with an iron glare. 'You know I'm right.'

Madge glared right back and stabbed a knitting needle in Peggy's direction. 'Did I say you were wrong? No, because you are not. But we know these things. What we need is not a lecture but a solution.'

'I know; I know. I just get so angry. The injustice of it all.' Peggy released a sharp puff of breath. 'Right. It's going to take us time to find the rapist. So I vote we deal with the rapscallion we know where to find.'

CHAPTER 9

wherein someone stores good wine badly

AFTER A SIMPLE DINNER at Peggy and Carole's, the four women got ready to leave. Baz wondered if Peggy might bring Cookie with them but, at the last minute, she sent Carole upstairs with him.

'Emmy and Amrita said they'd be happy to watch him for an hour or two,' Peggy said.

Baz frowned. 'Can he not be trusted on his own?' She couldn't imagine a better natured dog – he didn't seem the type to chew up the furniture or rummage through the rubbish.

'He's a big baby.' Peggy rolled her eyes. 'Cries like he's being murdered if he's left alone for so much as a minute. His size and his voice are enough to scare anyone off – but he doesn't seem to understand that.'

'Oh, poor lad,' Baz said.

'The idiot who had him first's fault.' Peggy shook her head with a look of disgust on her face. 'He tried to make that sweet boy into an attack dog.'

Baz leant against the wall as she pulled her shoes on. 'Oh,

that's dreadful. How horrible. Still, I'm glad he let you take Cookie off his hands.'

Peggy smirked. 'Well, I wouldn't exactly say he *let* me.'

Baz wasn't sure what that meant but it was time to head out.

The women stepped into the corridor and Peggy locked the door behind them. Once she was finished, she rubbed her hands together. 'Well then. Let's do this.'

The four set out together, walking or riding along New Cross Road. When they got to Watson's Street, they turned in, and then again on Baildon Street. It took a few minutes to find their destination amidst the warren of small blocks of flats.

Peggy and Baz parked their scooters out of the view from the road and joined the others at the building's entry. Peggy punched in the number. The buzzer sounded a few times before a young, male voice answered.

'Kevin? It's Peggy. I'm here.'

'Okay, I'll buzz you in. I sent you the flat number, right?'

Peggy leant close to the intercom board. 'You did.'

'Do you need me to come down to show you where to go?' Kevin's voice crackled over the speaker.

'We'll manage on our own, I think.'

'Thank you, Kevin,' added Madge. 'Very polite young man, I've always said.'

The door buzzed and the women walked in. The communal areas were shabby and minimalist but neatly maintained. The air smelt of cleaning product.

Peggy waved her cane towards the left. 'Stairs are that way.'

Carole set out resolutely in the direction Peggy had indicated. 'The universal gravity. We threw that in Einstein's face, I'll tell you.'

Both Peggy and Baz grimaced at the concrete steps. They looked at one another for a moment. After a few seconds,

Peggy inclined her head. 'Well, I guess we're doing this.' She set a bony hand on the handrail and began the long climb up two flights of stairs.

Baz took the handrail. She was awkward and slow going *up* stairs. Down was going to be much harder. But that was a problem for later.

'I'll bring up the rear,' Madge whispered. 'That way I can catch anyone who falls.'

'And what will you do once you've caught us, Madge?' Although Peggy had her back to her friends, Baz could envision the eyebrow that was almost certainly raised. 'I'll tell you what you'll do – you'll fall with us. But, I suppose, at least you'll cushion our fall. And why, pray tell, are you whispering?'

Baz heard Madge suck her teeth. 'We're on a covert mission. We've got to be secretive.'

'I see.' Peggy turned the corner halfway through the first flight of stairs and leant against the wall. 'And from whom are we secreting ourselves at this exact moment?' Baz suspected she was mainly talking as an excuse to take a rest before continuing onwards. Not that Baz was complaining.

Madge put her hands on her ample hips. 'You know this building is full of people just trying to live quiet, peaceable lives, right?'

'I'm not saying we should be shouting and carousing.' Putting a hand on the stair railing, Peggy looked up the next flight. 'Only pointing out that there's nothing inherently suspicious about four mature women chatting as they walk up a staircase in a building where they've been invited.'

Madge harrumphed – but quietly. 'I'm not sure the person we're paying a visit to would agree we've been invited.'

'A lawful resident of this building duly inv—'

Baz cleared her throat. 'Could we just focus on getting to the second floor, please?'

They carried on in silence and eventually emerged onto the floor of the man they'd come to visit.

'Now...' Peggy looked left and right before Carole tapped the wall.

Peering closely at the faded sign, Baz saw that it indicated which flat numbers were where.

The women took a moment to recover their collective breath and headed to the relevant door. Baz reached out a hand that was only slightly quivering and knocked twice.

'You've got the wrong place,' said a man from the other side of the door. 'I'm not looking to buy, donate, or be converted.'

'We've come to talk, Tom.' Baz wasn't sure how Peggy held her voice so steady. She didn't think she could have done the same.

Beyond the door, she heard shuffling footsteps followed by the unbolting of a lock. The door swung open a few inches and Tom's face appeared. 'What?'

But a few inches were all they needed. With four of them and only one of him, the ladies shoved their way in.

Flashing a grin that looked rather forced, Tom studied the group. 'Evening, ladies. Am I allowed to ask why you're in my home?'

'We need to have a chat, young man,' Madge said as she pushed past him.

Tom swallowed. 'I would've done a better job of tidying up if I'd known company was coming round.'

Baz recalled Kevin saying Tom had been raised by his grandmother. The way he responded to their presence, she wondered how much the women reminded him of her.

The flat was bland and unstylish yet expensively furnished. The walls were bare magnolia but the floor – a cheap laminate, Baz noted – was strewn with thick, plush rugs. She reached out a finger to touch the nearby sofa; it was – as she'd surmised –

soft Italian leather. A brand-name television perched on an assortment of milk crates. It was, naturally, much too large for the small space. The set-up was straddled by speakers that also bore a high-end brand name.

Tom spread his arms wide. 'Feels a bit late for a tea party, if I'm honest.'

Peggy was very nearly growling. 'Don't be cute, young man. I hate cute.'

'No one hates cute.' He flashed a dimply smile.

'I do,' she replied. 'And even if I were to enjoy it on occasion, I'm immune to the charms of men.'

'Ah,' he said. 'Well, in that case, don't I remind you of a beloved son?' He studied her face. 'Or grandson maybe?'

Peggy arched an eyebrow at him. Madge walked around the edges of the room, touching things and examining her fingers with a look of distaste.

Baz took a deep breath. 'I'm not, and never have been, immune to the charms of men.'

'You!' Tom looked at her, clearly spotting her for the first time since they'd arrived. 'What are *you* doing here?'

'I thought we could have a little chat about your girlfriend?' Baz studied Tom.

Tom smiled, though there was no warmth to it. 'My what?'

Baz breathed out through her nose. Lord give her strength. 'My granddaughter, Daisy? Until recently, she was your girlfriend. Perhaps that rings a bell.'

A dark look crossed Tom's face – there and then gone, all in a heartbeat. 'Well, I wouldn't go that far. We saw each other from time to time. But we were never in a *relationship*. It was purely sexual, you see.' He smiled coldly again. 'Sorry if that shocks you.'

Madge turned to face him. 'Really? Because we were under the impression it was more of a *financial* arrangement.'

'Look, I'm not sure what she told you—'

Peggy plucked a bottle of wine from a glass-fronted cabinet. 'She told us you were so broke you couldn't afford to feed your poor starving kids. And yet this cabinet here' – she waved a finger around, indicating the various bottles – 'contains at least 500 quid's worth of fine wines. And, for pity's sake, young man. Did no one tell you to store them on their sides? You'll dry out the corks like this.'

Madge tsked loudly.

'Look.' Tom raised his hands in self-defence. Baz wondered briefly where Carole had got to. 'Ladies, I can't help it if people like giving me gifts. No one's ever under any ... you know, thingy. They don't have to give me any—'

He stopped and looked away for a moment. 'Aha.' He returned his glance Baz's way. 'It was you what called the police on me, innit? You mad old cow. I blamed Daisy – but it was you all along.' He pointed at Baz. 'They come round here the other day, asking all sorts of questions.'

Before Baz could reply, Carole appeared behind Tom. She thrust her left arm under his armpit and up around his throat in a sort of half-Nelson move. Baz saw a flash of metal as Carole's right arm punched him in the side of the head. Still gripping him tightly, she appeared to massage his ear.

Tom squeaked and then sort of gurgled, falling to the floor.

No, not punched. And definitely not massaged.

Carole pulled her long, metal knitting needle from the man's ear, trailing a slick but chunky line of red. She laughed lightly, like the sound of tinkling bells. 'What fun! I haven't done that in ages.'

Baz got down on her knees – her ruined knees – and felt for the man's breath. None. She listened for a heartbeat. Nothing. She tried to scream but no sound would come, so she began compressions.

Carole studied her needle, then pulled a hankie from her pocket and wiped it clean. 'If you get just the right angle, you'll sever the brainstem. A tricky manoeuvre, but neat as a pin if you know what you're doing. I keep the point on my needle sharp, so it glides in like a hot knife through butter.'

'What have you done?' Although she still wanted to scream, Baz's words were soft. 'This isn't what we came here for.' She halted compressions and breathed into Tom's mouth.

Peggy studied her. 'Isn't it?'

'No,' said Baz firmly. Finally able to put some force into her words. 'We're not killers.'

Madge and Peggy exchanged another one of those infuriating glances. Carole opened her knitting bag and removed a velvet sheath, into which she slid the needle.

Baz squared her shoulders as she continued compressions, still trying to think up a way out of this mess. 'We came here to talk to him.' Perhaps Carole could plead diminished capacity. But no judge was going to believe the rest of them were anything other than completely competent.

Madge sucked her teeth. 'To what end?'

'To tell him to... Well, to persuade him to...' Baz shuddered as she heard a rib crack beneath her. 'Now what are we going to do?' Her voice sounded shrill even to her own ears.

But Carole had her phone out and was holding it to her ear – a macabre echo of what she'd done moments earlier. 'Hello, love. How are you doing?'

There was a pause in Carole's one-sided conversation, during which Baz was still doing compressions and trying to figure out what to do next. She'd tell the cops it was an accident. They'd believe that – wouldn't they? Four more puffs of air into Tom's mouth.

'Oh, wonderful,' said Carole into her phone brightly. 'Hey, listen. Do you still have that removals service you use?' A brief pause. 'Yes, that one.' Baz pressed down on Tom's chest twice more and then Carole continued, 'Excellent. Yes, I'm going to need them tonight.' She looked behind herself, to where a pool of blood was visible beneath Tom's head. Baz frowned – what a shame to disfigure that beautiful Turkish rug.

'The cleaners? Yes, I should think so.' Carole rattled off the address of the flat they'd invaded. 'There's a potted cedar by the front door. I think it might be a fake. You know, plastic. Shame. I'll put the cedar in the wilderness – the acacia and the myrtle and the olive tree. I'll place the juniper in the desert.'

Baz almost lost her dinner as Carole scratched her head with the end of the velvet sheath. 'Anyhow, dear, I'll leave the keys under that. We should be out of the way in another fifteen or twenty. We'll be long gone before your fellows arrive.'

There was a final pause in the conversation and then Carole said, 'Excellent, thanks, love. Yes, no worries. They can send me the bill in the usual manner – though there should be more than enough here to offset it. Cheers, see you soon. Ta-ta.' She clicked the button to hang up and then slid the phone – and the murder weapon – back into her bag.

Baz sighed, letting her shoulders sag. It occurred to her she'd stopped compressions at some point and was now simply sitting on a corpse, which seemed disrespectful. She pinched her lips together, in a desperate bid to forestall a flood of tears.

Peggy and Madge both offered Baz their hands. 'Come on,' said Peggy. 'Let's get you up and out of here. You can fall apart once you're safely back in your own home. Not here.'

Baz thought about it for a moment, unsure whether to accept the proffered assistance or not. But, of course, in the end, she did. What else was she going to do? Sit there astride a dead man all night?

Peggy grabbed a couple of bottles of wine from the cabinet and deposited them in her handbag.

The four women slowly climbed back down the stairs with far less conversation than they'd made on the way up. By the time they opened the front door and stepped outside, the night had developed a distinct chill.

Baz and Peggy collected their mobility scooters. 'That reminds me,' Baz whispered. 'When the body's discovered, someone will remember having seen us. Certainly, if nothing else, Kevin—'

'Let me stop you right there.' Peggy got herself seated on her scooter and turned the key to start the engine. 'Nothing will be discovered,' she whispered.

Baz spoke directly into Peggy's ear. 'Not tonight perhaps. But eventu—'

'Not ever. Carole's people know what they're doing.'

'But—'

'For pity's sake. We can't have this conversation here,' Peggy hissed. 'Let's get you home. We can talk through what happens next once we're safe from prying ears and eyes.'

Peggy steered her scooter back out onto the footpath. With a gazillion and one questions still whirling around in her head, Baz followed. Daisy was out with her girlfriends this evening, so they would at least have some privacy.

'Slight change of plans, ladies.' Peggy pulled ahead of Madge and Carole. 'We're all going to Baz's for a little nightcap.'

It must have taken them about a quarter of an hour to get to Baz's, though she was unaware of the passage of time. They must have had to wait for the lights to change – at New Cross Road and again at Brookmill Road. But she had no recollection of it.

The concierge looked up from her desk. 'Ladies, you're out late this eve. I hope you've been having fun.'

Baz swallowed and forced herself to mind her manners, even though the world was spinning. 'Good evening, Jessica.

How are you?' She was sure there was a solid mass in her throat.

'I'm all good, Baz. Anything you need? You look a bit peaky.'

Bless the girl. 'Thank you, dear. My friends are coming upstairs for a cup of tea. Would it be all right if Peggy leaves her mobility scooter with you for a little bit? She won't be long, but there isn't space in the flat for both mine and hers. Or the lift, for that matter.' It felt like her voice was coming from another realm.

'Of course, my lovely.' Jessica smiled and studied Baz's face. 'But are you sure everything's all right?'

Baz opened her mouth to reply but no words came out.

'She's fine,' Madge said. 'Thank you.'

Peggy dismounted her scooter and rested a hand on Baz's shoulder. 'Just needs a cuppa and a good night's rest.'

Baz steered her scooter towards the lift. Peggy reached out and pressed the button.

As soon as they were in the flat, Baz collapsed onto her usual chair. Peggy made straight for the kitchen. Baz heard the tap running, the kettle being flipped on, and the cupboards being rummaged through.

Madge pulled an ottoman over and perched in front of Baz. She reached out and took Baz's hands in her own strong, rough ones. Baz looked down at her pale hands wrapped in the rich brown of Madge's.

'It's strange,' Baz heard herself say. 'For the past twenty minutes it's been all I could do to keep myself from crying. I fought to keep the tears at bay. Peggy said I could cry once we got here but not until, so I held myself together. And yet now that we're here ... the tears won't come.'

Madge gripped her hands tightly. 'They will. For now, you're in shock. The tears will come. You will mourn. You will lament.

And you'll grieve for the life that ended tonight – for the man he could have been. You'll question your own actions a thousand times over. And when you do, I hope you will come to see that we did what was necessary. I'm not saying it was good or even right. But it was *necessary*. That young man was a menace to our community.'

Peggy placed a mug in Baz's hands. There was something comforting about holding such a big, bowl-shaped mug, especially filled as it was with strong, hot tea. Builder's tea. Baz let the steam wash over her.

'If he'd shown remorse,' Peggy said, 'Carole's needle would have stayed in her bag. If the police would have done their job, we'd never have gone there. But Madge is right. What we did, we did for the good of our community. Drink up.'

Baz took a long sip of her tea.

Carole came and stood beside her. 'First one's always the hardest.'

Madge stood up. 'Get that down you. You'll feel better for it.'

Baz did as instructed.

For the second time that night, both Peggy and Madge offered their arms to her. 'Now, let's get you to bed before that kicks in.'

A deep, aching sense of dread washed over Baz. 'Have you—'

'Yes,' Peggy replied.

'—murdered me?'

'What?' Peggy took hold of Baz's arms. More gently than she had feared, though. 'Of course not. Don't be such a ninny.'

Madge put her tongue to her teeth.

'Don't you dare!' Baz wagged a finger in Madge's face. 'Don't you dare suck your teeth at me.'

Madge closed her mouth and appeared to consider her next

words. 'Why would you even suggest such a thing?' She looked indignant.

'We have just come back from the house of a man who was most definitely alive when we arrived. And when we left, he was not.' Baz could hear the pitch of her voice rising to uncomfortable levels. 'So don't you dare imply that asking whether I'm about to be murdered makes me a daft old woman.'

'Relax,' said Peggy in a tone that would not have made anyone the slightest bit calmer. 'No one's getting murdered tonight.' She cocked her head. 'Well, no one else. And never anyone who doesn't one hundred per cent deserve it.'

'And you, my dear,' Madge took Baz by the arm and began to lead her towards the bedroom, 'definitely do not deserve it.'

'Which one's yours?' Peggy indicated the four doors ahead of them. One of them was the bathroom and one was a cupboard. One was Daisy's room. And... 'It's that one. Hang on. If you're not murdering me, then what did you mean, "Before that kicks in"?'

'Oh, I did drug you.' Peggy opened Baz's bedroom door.

Baz raised her hand to wag a finger at Peggy but Peggy brushed her hand away. 'Just a light sedative. It's for your own good. You'll benefit from a deep and dreamless sleep tonight, I promise. And tomorrow you'll think about what happened and what you want to do next.'

Peggy and Madge guided Baz to the bed and sat her down and then left. As Madge shut the light off, she turned to face Baz. 'Good night, dear. Sleep well.'

Baz was too stunned to respond. The women closed the bedroom door. A few moments later, she heard the flat door close.

And then finally, alone in the dark, the tears came.

CHAPTER 10

in which everything is fine, actually

TWO WEEKS LATER, Peggy settled herself into her usual chair at Wellbeloved. She necked her espresso, then slid her laptop from its bag and placed it on her lap. With the screen open before her, she re-read the last words she'd written.

'I think we have passed the stage of being merely friends – don't you think?' John asked him, half expecting an answer but not putting his hopes on it. 'Should you not, by this stage, be taking an interest in my interests?'

Peggy stared at the words for a while, allowing Sam's response to take shape in her mind. After a few moments, she placed her fingers on the keys and began typing.

'I would prefer not to spend all my time rolling in the dirt, no matter the company.'

Back in the here and now, the bell chimed as the café's door opened. Two black-clad figures walked in. One headed for the front counter and the other ducked through to the room where the women sat. 'Morning, Granny. Morning, Aunties.'

Madge looked up from her knitting, pretending she hadn't noticed her grandson walk in. 'Young Peter! What a pleasant surprise. Where's that handsome partner of yours?'

Peter bent to kiss his grandmother on the cheek. 'Mike's just getting us coffee.'

'What on Earth are you doing in here then, young man? You're the junior. Fetching drinks is your responsibility.' Madge shook her head. 'I know your daddy raised you better than this, because I raised him.'

'Oh, don't chide the boy,' said the oily officer as he joined them. 'I offered to get the drinks in while he came to say hello to you.' With a wink, he added, 'Now you're making me feel guilty for trying to do a nice thing.'

PC West raised a bottle of grapefruit juice to his mouth and took a long swig, his Adam's apple bobbing. Peggy watched her friends' reactions with disgust – even Carole was licking her lips. Peggy sometimes thought you could put a uniform on a pig and the brainwashed masses would swoon over it. That pig would prance about like a strutting pheasant – if she could mix her metaphors – basking in all the fawning attention. *Ooh, that was a good phrase.* She added it to the 'to be used later' file in her book.

When he'd finished his seductive display, Mike turned to Peter. 'The lovely young lady at the counter said she'd bring our coffees over in a few minutes.'

Peter nodded. He looked like he wanted to say something.

Peggy assumed it was fear of being shot down by Madge's sharp tongue that prevented him.

Madge waved a knitting needle in the handsome officer's direction. 'You're looking a lovely golden brown today, young man. You've certainly not been getting any sun around here lately.'

Mike smiled. 'No, ma'am. Thank you, ma'am. Just back from a couple weeks' leave.'

Peggy was spared the inanity of insipid tales of his no doubt tedious holiday by the arrival of Olena, who stood in the doorway with two takeaway mugs. 'Mike? I've got your coffees here?'

Even the young were not immune, Peggy noticed. Olena smiled but glanced away, as if she were too shy to look the man in the face. Fighting the urge to roll her eyes, Peggy looked down at her computer and carried on typing.

The kiss was light and soft. Like a feather that barely had time to reach the ground before a breeze swept it off. And yet, it left an imprint. 'What was that for?'

The bell above the door wouldn't have been sufficient to jerk Peggy back from her story. But the blasted voice that followed it did the trick.

'Wagwan, ladies?' Clive clutched his hand to his chest and affected a swoon. 'Oh, my my my! And who is your handsome friend? What a delight you are!' He reached out to shake the officer's hand. Or perhaps to allow him to kiss it. Who could be certain with Clive?

'PC Mike West.' He shook the proffered hand. 'Delighted to make your acquaintance...?'

Clive batted his eyelashes like a besotted schoolgirl. 'Likewise, I'm sure. I'm Clive – Clive Chen. I'm the leader of Deptford's premier local crafters' circle, the Purly Queens.' Both Peggy and Madge scoffed noisily at that. 'That's purly with a U, you understand.'

Before Mike could respond, Carole looked up. 'Oh, Clive, I've been meaning to ask you... You know what a dachshund is, right?'

Clive furrowed his brow and glanced sideways to see if there was a joke he wasn't in on. When no one came to his rescue, he said, 'Yes, it's a small dog?'

Carole shook her head disgustedly. 'What? No, I said a dachshund! You do know what a dachshund is, right?'

Clive spoke more confidently this time. 'It's a small dog. A sausage dog.'

Carole waved her needles at him in a dismissive fashion. 'You're an idiot!' She turned to Mike and Peter. 'You know the first blood transfusion in 1852 in America? They would take the blood of a newborn baby and drill holes in its head, so it would never gain muscle control. It's all just mad, isn't it?'

Mike looked a question at Peter, who responded by shrugging.

Wagging a finger, Clive fixed Carole with a piercing gaze. 'You're a cheeky one, Carole. You want us to think you're as mad as a box of frogs.' He sucked air through his teeth – Madge's favourite expression of disapproval. 'I ain't falling for it.'

Mike clapped Clive on the shoulder and nodded at the women. 'Well, it's been lovely chatting with you, ladies. And Clive. Alas, I'm going to have to tear your favourite constable away from you. Time, tide, and criminals wait for no one. We'd best be getting back to work, trying to keep our streets safe from those who would flout His Majesty's laws.'

Peggy lost the battle and her eyes rolled so far back she feared her retinas would detach.

———

Not long afterwards, Peggy glanced up from her keyboard. 'Well, well, well. Look what the cat dragged in.' Outside Well-beloved's window, Baz was on her scooter, heading to her normal parking spot.

Carole was crocheting a pair of human lungs. 'Well, of course you can't tell the difference between foxes and ginger cats. But then it was just a load of rabbit fur. And they do talk such a load of rubbish.'

Madge looked up and nodded approvingly. 'I wondered how long it would take her to come back.'

Peggy clicked to save the file she was working on. 'Really? Because I'll be honest... I was at least halfway convinced we'd never see Baz again.'

The bell over the door chimed softly as Baz walked in. Before heading to the front counter, she stuck her head into the café's second room. 'Morning, ladies. Anyone for a top-up?'

Peggy approved of the lack of fanfare. 'I'll have another espresso, please, Baz.'

Baz nodded. 'Of course. Back in a jiff.'

Peggy returned her attention to the book she was writing.

———

'And what if I decide never to come back to England?'

———

She stretched her fingers out and typed a few more sentences while Baz ordered her tea.

———

John almost rolled his eyes at Sam's outburst. Almost. If there was one thing he knew for certain, it was that the man before him could be over-sensitive when he was feeling insecure. 'You'll be back.'

Sam toyed with his gloves. 'Why? Since you're so smug and sure in my affairs and actions now, I mean.'

It was quiet enough in the shop that Peggy could hear Baz having a friendly chat with Olena at the front counter. Not what they were saying, mind, only that they sounded friendly.

After a few minutes, Baz ducked through the doorway and took her seat. The ladies had set it out for her every morning over the past two weeks, hoping she'd be there.

Baz pulled her embroidery bag to her lap and removed her work. 'Chilly this morning.'

Madge nodded. 'It is that.'

'Might rain later,' Peggy said without taking her eyes off her laptop.

John allowed a coy smile to cross his face. 'Because I'm here, not there. You must bear that in mind.'

The women worked on their respective projects in silence. Beneath the table, Cookie played with his anatomically correct crocheted heart. Occasionally, he shifted position. Once, he lucked out when someone at a nearby table dropped a few crumbs of their cake.

After nearly an hour of sitting in peace, Baz looked up. 'How is your neighbour, Peggy? Emily, wasn't it?'

Peggy looked out the window. 'Emmy. She's doing well, thank you. As well as can be expected. She's had a couple of counselling sessions at the health centre. She took a few days off her classes but she's been back for almost a week now. Carole and I check in on her every few days.'

'I baked a cake,' said Carole.

Peggy nodded. 'She did.' What she left out was their argument over how the cake should be decorated. Carole's original design was probably a bit too ... graphic for the occasion.

Baz continued her embroidery for a while, though Peggy could see she was aching to say something. If she didn't speak soon, Peggy would prompt her.

But in the end, she didn't need to.

Baz looked up. 'You know there's not been another attack in the area for ... almost two weeks? It seems that the attack on your young friend was the last.'

Ah.

'Mmm hmm.' Madge didn't look up. 'I've not heard anything lately.'

Peggy closed her laptop, leaving John wondering how Sam would respond. 'It does seem that he's taking a bit of a break from his activities.'

Baz had an optimistic look in her eye. 'Or, you know, maybe something happened to him?'

'I see.' Peggy leant forwards in her chair, gripping the armrests with her fingers. Today's nail polish was a fire engine red. She enjoyed the way it clashed with the pink of her hair. 'And you think that ... something ... happened to the perpetrator – do you?' She hauled herself up to her feet. 'Popping to the loo. Back in a mo.' She motioned for Cookie to lie back down.

For once, she didn't actually have to go. She was just buying herself time to think. Over the past two weeks, she and Madge had been asking around about this so-called Goldsmiths Groper. The loo door was locked, so she stood in the small corridor, waiting her turn.

The only direct contact they'd had with a victim was Emmy. And she hadn't seen much. Oh, she'd been through a hellish nightmare of an ordeal – but she hadn't seen her attacker. She'd heard him speak and had described him as incongruously charming – behaving as though they were in some sort of relationship and this was a consensual assignation.

Bastard!

Peggy had seen the rogue with her own two eyes. And yet she couldn't provide anything more than a vague description. Roughly average height. Average build. She couldn't even say whether he was black, white, or turquoise.

Well, barring incredibly exceptionally unexpected circumstances, she was pretty sure she could eliminate turquoise men from the running.

A man emerged from the café's small loo and smiled at her as he walked past. Peggy scowled at him – for all she knew, he could be the very man they sought.

She made her way in and lowered herself onto the toilet. What if Baz's wishful thinking were the reality? Could Tom Jackson really have been the Goldsmiths Groper?

Think it through logically. The attacks had been going on for four months – which lined up with when Kevin said Tom was released from prison.

The victims and witnesses all seemed to agree that the man sounded local. Tom was as local as they come. They said the man had spoken charmingly, which fit with Tom as well.

And so far, there had been no more attacks since Tom met his fate.

Huh.

Peggy finished up, washed her hands, and returned to her seat with the other ladies.

'Baz was just sharing a little bit of gossip,' said Madge.

Baz nodded. 'Daisy's ex-boyfriend...' She cast her eyes around anxiously. 'You remember him, right?'

Peggy inhaled slowly. 'Yes, Baz. I believe we all remember what terrible taste your lovely granddaughter has in men.'

Baz tittered. 'Daisy had Jenna over for dinner last night. You recall that young woman who first introduced us to the possibility of a predator on the loose?' Peggy and Madge nodded. 'Jenna told us that, apparently, Tom has up and moved to France.'

'France, eh?' Peggy chuckled.

Madge made a slight smirk. 'Good for him.'

They worked in silence again for a bit. Peggy studied her screen. She tried to think of how Sam would respond but nothing was coming to her. After a few minutes, she had to admit to herself that her heart – and more importantly her mind – was elsewhere.

Slamming the lid of her laptop, she looked up. 'I've been thinking about what you said, Baz. And perhaps you're right. Perhaps we killed two birds with—' The terrified look on Baz's face said she didn't appreciate Peggy's choice of metaphor. 'Excuse me. Perhaps we solved two problems with a single action.'

Baz leant closer and half whispered, half hissed, 'You agree that *he* was *him*?'

Peggy sighed. 'I think there is a possibility that Tom Jackson, who, as we all know, recently left the UK, may have been the predator the press calls so euphemistically the Goldsmiths Groper.'

Baz let out a long slow breath and with it she seemed to deflate. 'Huh.'

———

THAT NIGHT, Peggy made ratatouille for dinner and Carole made a cake in the shape of a human torso – without skin or muscles but with anatomically correct organs. Afterwards, they watched the latest episode of the newest BBC crime drama. Carole went to bed at around ten and Peggy switched to watching old episodes of *Law & Order*.

Just after midnight, Peggy took Cookie out for his final walk of the day. Ever since that fateful night a few weeks ago when she'd been too late to save Emmy, she'd taken to carrying a small knife with her. She hadn't needed it – but woe betide anyone who thought her helpless simply because she was old.

Mind you, people tended to steer clear of her on account of Cookie. She chuckled aloud at the thought of that. 'Fat lot of good you'd be in a fight, mate,' she said to him as he cocked his leg against a new model BMW. 'No offence.'

Clearly not offended, Cookie finished his business and resumed walking. Peggy looked around at the neighbourhood she loved so much. Maybe they really were safe from this menace.

Ah, well. There'd be a new trouble soon enough. The battle to keep their community safe was a never-ending one.

CHAPTER 11

wherein two people have very bad days, separately

AFTER A LIGHT LUNCH, Baz decided to head up the road to yoga class. Despite her bravado, she still wasn't feeling entirely comfortable with ... well, with the events of two weeks previous: the night she and her friends paid a visit to Tom Jackson. She understood what Madge had said about things being necessary. It was clear the police weren't going to do anything about his activities.

And now it appeared he may indeed have been the Goldsmiths Groper. Well, that certainly helped soothe Baz's conscience. Somewhat.

Between starting hormone therapy, the end of her marriage, the move to London, and ... well, everything, she felt like a churning ball of emotional turmoil. She burst into tears at the slightest provocation. Sometimes they were tears of frustration, sometimes they were happy tears, sad tears, guilty tears, or just tears of exhaustion.

The yoga would help her find some inner peace, she reckoned. And it may have ... if she'd made it there.

She hadn't actually gone that far. The intersection nearest

her building was notorious for traffic accidents. Pedestrians and cars heading westbound had an advanced green while cars that were turning south still faced a red. Not that drivers paid any heed to the lights. She'd witnessed so many near accidents since moving to this neighbourhood that she'd been considering writing a sternly worded letter to the local council.

And wouldn't you know it, on this particular afternoon, she'd waited for the walk light to turn green and then headed out across the road on her scooter. Only a driver turning onto Brookmill Road had picked that moment to run the red. He'd slammed straight into her rear corner. Fortunately, he hadn't been going that fast. Fast enough to wreck her scooter ... not enough to do much real damage to Baz herself. Though she did make a bit of a mess of her good knee. And she'd torn her favourite dress.

The driver was apologetic – he wasn't familiar with the area and hadn't seen the red light. A whole host of passers-by had stopped to check on her. The driver promised to pay for the replacement scooter and to have her dress mended. A very kind young man dragged her broken mobility scooter back to the apartment building while his husband, a nurse, offered his elbow to Baz.

All things considered, the whole thing was as civil and pleasant as a nearly life-altering accident could possibly be. She chided herself for being so shaken up. No one had been harmed. The driver had left her his name, number, and all the relevant details. The mobility scooter company had promised to send her a rental model by Thursday.

The young gentlemen who'd walked her home – Mick and Rick – ushered her all the way up to the flat. They even stayed long enough for Rick the nurse to clean and bandage her knee and for Mick the builder to make her a cup of tea. They left her with their numbers, an ice pack on her knee, and a pot of tea by her side.

She decided to take it easy the rest of the day. She drank her tea and settled in front of the television. At dinner time, she ordered a takeaway.

And at ten o'clock on the nose, she dragged herself off to bed. It was unseasonably warm, so she pushed the covers off and made herself as comfy as her swollen knee would allow. She'd just opened her book and found the place she'd left off when the entryphone sounded.

She ignored it. It was late. No one would be calling her at this hour. The good thing about living in a building with a concierge was that these nuisance calls didn't happen often.

Nuisance calls don't happen in a building with a concierge.

She hauled herself out of bed as quickly as she could. Grabbing her cane, she made her way to the door – with both legs now hindering her progress. 'I'm coming, I'm coming,' she muttered although no one could hear her. 'Shouldn't Daisy be home by now?'

By the time she got to the door, the buzzer had long since stopped ringing. She called down to the front desk but got the generic voicemail greeting that said the on-duty attendant was away from their desk. 'Please leave a message or try again in a few minutes.'

Too sore and tired from the short walk to turn around and go back to bed, Baz leant against the wall, considering her options. She didn't think she had the strength to hold herself upright very long, even with the cane. Her right knee couldn't support her weight for very long at the best of times. And now her left knee was bruised and swollen like a mottled beachball.

That left her with two options: shuffle to the nearest chair in the living room or begin the longer journey down the hall back to bed. If she chose the chair, she'd be able to get the weight off her poor knees in less than a minute. But she might be stuck there until Daisy got home and could help get her back to bed.

Mind you, if she didn't make a decision in the next few seconds, her knees were going to buckle under her. And then she'd be stuck on the cold, hard floor all night.

Actually... If she got down on the floor, she could use her arms to slide herself—

The sound of a key in the door caught her attention. 'Oh, Daisy! I'm so glad you're home. I don't want to worry you but I—'

When the door swung inwards, it wasn't Daisy she saw, but Jessica, the concierge. And the look on her face said this wasn't a social call. As the door opened wider, a second person came into view. Daisy. She was shaking.

Old habits die hard. Baz had spent more than half her life working for the police. She may have been a civilian investigator rather than an officer. But she'd taken part in interviews on occasion – or even just sat with the victims.

Injured joints temporarily forgotten, she went into work mode now. After placing her arm around Daisy's waist, Baz worked with Jessica to help Daisy into the living room.

They got her to the sofa and lowered her down. When Baz tried to release her, Daisy clung to her arm like a vice grip, nails digging into her grandmother's arm. 'Please, Nan. Please. Don't leave me.'

They hadn't switched the lights on but the ambient light from the street nine storeys down was enough to see one another. Baz looked a question at Jessica as she spoke soothing nothings to her granddaughter. 'Shh, shh. I'm not going anywhere. There, there, my dear. Nan's got you now.' With her chin, she beckoned Jessica to her other side. The young woman came round and dropped to her knees on Baz's free side. 'What happened?' Baz whispered.

Jessica leant close to Baz's ear. 'I think she was attacked.'

'Attacked?' Baz's throat closed as the bottom dropped out of her stomach. 'Was she...?'

Jessica shrugged and shook her head. 'I'm not sure.'

Daisy's tremors began to ease off. 'I wasn't raped, if that's what you're asking.' Her voice was so soft it was barely audible even to Baz as she held her tight. 'But not for lack of effort on his part.'

Baz clutched the girl even tighter. 'What happened?'

Daisy stood up, still shivering. 'I need to... I need to... I don't know. Maybe I just need to keep moving.' She smacked her lips and made a sort of gagging sound. 'No. Water.'

Baz started to ask if she wanted a hot bath, but Daisy flew across the room to the kitchen sink. She poured herself a pint glass of water, swirled it around in her mouth, and then spat. As she repeated the process a few more times, Baz looked another question at Jessica.

'I don't know what happened.' Jessica shook her head. 'I heard a noise outside, so I went to check. At first, I thought maybe it was foxes – you know how they scream sometimes. But it was close. Foxes don't normally come so close to the building. Or at least, they're quiet when they do – know what I mean?'

In the kitchen, Daisy poured another glass of water. This one, she drank. All in one go.

'When I got around the side of the building,' Jessica continued, 'I saw a man running off. And I found Daisy.' Her voice trailed off as Daisy returned from the kitchen with another full glass of water. She dropped onto the sofa and collapsed into Baz.

The shakes and nervous energy had faded. When she spoke,

her voice was stronger than it had been before. 'I was at Jenna's. We were working on a plan for the next round of self-defence classes. It was getting late and I was tired, so I took the bus. I mean, I could've walked but ... I didn't. Maybe I'd have been safer if I did.'

She shook her head. 'I took the bus. I got off just around the corner and walked through Broadway Fields. I thought I saw someone following me but ... I don't know. Maybe I assumed it was my imagination.'

Daisy leant into Baz, who put her arms around her. 'He jumped me when I was behind the building. Right there in front of all those flats. He asked me what I liked and if doing it in public turned me on.' She raised her hand to her mouth again, like she was afraid she might be sick. Baz thought she might be as well.

'He said he understood what I wanted – what I needed. Like, the whole time he was attacking me, he was talking to me like we were on a date or something. It was just so freaking weird.'

She shook her head and scowled. 'He had his arm around my throat and I struggled to get into a position where I could defend myself. Dude wasn't just strong – he had training. Like, martial arts or something. He knew all the moves I was going to make and he countered them. He's trained and he fights dirty. Honestly, I know it sounds weird but at the time all I could think was that if we were just sparring, it would have been an awesome workout. As it was...' She sagged like a deflating balloon.

There was a pause and Baz thought Daisy might be all talked out for now. She had said she hadn't been raped, hadn't she? But she'd clearly been traumatised by what had happened.

Daisy took a drink of her water. But then instead of swallowing, she ran to the sink and spat. Cupping her hands beneath the tap, she rinsed her mouth again and again.

When she returned, she opened her mouth to continue speaking but then burst into giggles instead. Baz had seen it before; you couldn't always predict how victims – no, survivors – would react. Shock hit people in different ways and at different times. Hysterical fits of laughter weren't all that uncommon.

Jessica put a hand on Daisy's arm. 'What—'

Baz looked Jessica in the eye and shook her head. *Let her process things in her own time*, she thought, willing Jessica to understand her psychically.

They waited a few more minutes in silence but finally Daisy's laughter slowed and then stopped. Baz handed her a tissue and she blew her nose.

'I bit him,' she said before chewing her lip as though she feared a return of the giggles.

Jessica's eyes widened. 'On the...?' Her jaw fell slack.

Daisy brought her fist to her mouth. The edges of her eyes crinkled. 'No, no, no.' She waved her right hand around. 'On the arm. It was the only thing I could do in the end. He had such a strong hold on me that none of the normal moves worked. He was behind me and his arm was around my throat. I bit him so hard I—'

Her hand flew up to cover her mouth and she ran for the sink a third time. This time, she was violently sick. Baz and Jessica followed her – though Jessica moved noticeably quicker. With Baz holding her hair back, Daisy vomited and retched until she had nothing left. And then she dry-heaved a few times. She reached up to her shoulder and squeezed Baz's hand before rinsing her mouth out. 'I think I actually swallowed a chunk of his flesh. Every time I remember it, I...' She spat once more into the sink, running the tap to clear it away.

Her shoulders fell and she walked back over to the sofa, with Jessica at her side. Baz used the counter to support herself. When she reached the end, she let go ... and promptly tumbled to the ground, landing hard on her bum.

Both Jessica and Daisy ran to her; Jessica grabbed her under the arms and lifted her back up. Daisy flicked a small lamp on. Together they helped Baz back to the sofa and lifted her swollen leg up onto the coffee table. Baz felt horribly guilty. She was built like a stack of breeze blocks; no one should have to carry her.

'What the hell happened to you?' Daisy's nostrils flared and her voice was raised. 'You've just let me sit here and blubber on about how I *wasn't* raped, when all the while you've ... you've... What happened?' She waved her hands at Baz's knee, which had ballooned up like a ... well, like a balloon.

'It's nothing,' Baz said. 'You were attacked. I was just hit by – well, it was a very minor traffic collision. No harm done.' She waved a hand dismissively.

'No harm done?' Daisy shrieked. 'No harm done! Look at you. Your leg looks like a tree trunk. Did you at least go to the hospital?' She leapt off the sofa and began pacing in small circles.

Baz raised her hands in a placating gesture. 'A nurse examined me. I'm fine. He bandaged the wound. I took some painkillers. Everything's fine – I promise.'

Jessica furrowed her brow. 'I should go.' She stood up and walked backwards towards the door.

Baz started to get up, grimaced, and sat back down. 'Thank you, Jessica. You've gone so far beyond the call of duty tonight. I'm truly grateful for your help.'

Daisy brushed herself off and walked Jessica to the door. 'Thank you. Honestly. I've no idea what I would've done tonight if you'd not been there.'

Baz heard the two of them having a whispered conversation. Daisy hugged the much shorter woman and then closed the door behind her. She bolted the lock and slid the chain into place. When she was finished, she came back to the sofa and dropped down next to Baz. 'I'm so sorry, Nan. I feel like a jerk, banging on about my problems when you were actually hurt and I didn't even notice it.'

'Honey, you mustn't talk like that.' Baz put her arm around her granddaughter – the person she loved most in all the world. 'I'm sorry I didn't tell you about my accident. I would have told you eventually – but you've had a very traumatic evening. I didn't want to add to that.'

Daisy rested her head on Baz's shoulder. 'I guess we've both had a pretty crappy day, eh?' She leant over and flipped the lamp off. 'I suppose we really should call the police. But do you think it would be okay if we waited until the morning? I'm too tired to deal with it right now.'

There was no DNA to collect – it had all gone down the drain. Baz stroked Daisy's hair. 'Of course, honey.'

They sat together on the sofa with only the ambient light from outside and the soft susurrus of traffic far below. After a while, Daisy stood up and held out an arm for Baz. 'Would it be all right if I slept with you tonight, Nan?'

Baz smiled. 'Of course, dear. I'm afraid you'll have to help me get there, though.'

CHAPTER 12

in which a vegan turns cannibal

WHEN BAZ AWOKE at around seven thirty, Daisy was curled into a tiny ball on the other side of the bed, breathing softly. As quietly as she could, Baz retrieved her phone from her nightstand to text the girls.

BAZ

> Morning, ladies. I can't make it this morning. Unfortunately, Daisy was

She paused for a moment and then deleted the last three words. She sent the message and tried again.

BAZ

> I do have news about our local problem.

No, she thought. *That's not right.* She deleted the words and sat with her fingers hovering over the face of the phone.

BAZ

> ...

But no words came to her. After a few moments, she shook her head and tried again.

BAZ

> My mobility scooter is out of commission until tomorrow afternoon and I'm not up to the walk.

Immediately, a reply popped up.

MADGE

> Peggy will bring you hers at nine o'clock this morning. She can do without it for a few days. Be ready at the front desk of your building.

Baz lifted the duvet and looked at her injured leg. Her freshly injured left leg — as opposed to the right leg with its chronic injury. She sat up and put her feet on the floor, then pulled herself upright — and promptly fell back to the bed.

'Ow!' She tried to keep her voice low to avoid waking Daisy. But to no avail. Daisy sat up and looked around groggily.

'Morning, honey. Sorry to wake you. How are you feeling?'

Daisy held her hair back from her face with one hand and used the other to wipe the sleep from her eyes. She yawned. 'Better than you by the sounds of it.'

'Touché.' Baz ran her hand down her swollen leg.

'I take it you're having trouble getting up.' Daisy sprang out of bed with the resiliency of youth. She walked around to the other side of the bed and held a hand out for Baz. 'C'mon. I'll help you get to the bathroom.'

Baz held a hand up. 'Just one sec. Need to fire off a quick text first.'

'Sure.' Daisy lowered her hand and walked to the window. 'Let me know when you're ready.'

BAZ

Peggy, I don't like to put you on the spot. If you are able to spare the scooter for a couple of days, though, I would be grateful. Also, if it's okay, would you mind bringing it up to the flat, please? I'm not in any fit state to get down to the lobby on my own.

MADGE

She'll be fine. Don't worry.

BAZ

Thank you, Madge. Peggy, let me know, would you?

MADGE

She'll be there. Nine o'clock sharp. Be ready.

BAZ

Thank you, my lovelies.

She set her phone back on the nightstand. 'Sorry, Daisy. When you're ready.'

Daisy helped her up and supported her the short distance to the en suite. 'I'll wait out here so I can help you to the living room. You can tell me what happened while I make us breakfast, yeah?'

Baz smiled – grimacing only slightly with the pain of walking. 'You're a good girl, Daisy.'

———

HALF AN HOUR LATER, Daisy delivered plates of pancakes and veggie sausages to the table. She made another trip to the kitchen and then dropped into her own chair, placing the maple syrup and vegan butter in the centre of the table.

'Thank you, honey. This looks lovely.' In theory, Baz wasn't vegan. Daisy was, though. In practice, that meant Baz was mostly vegan. A true Albertan, her ex-husband had struggled with the change in diet. But Baz never really minded.

Daisy dressed her pancake and then sliced off a mouthful. Just before biting into it, she said, 'So? What really happened yesterday?'

'Oh, it was nothing.' Baz waved her fork in a dismissive gesture. 'Really. Not compared to what you went through.'

Daisy swallowed. 'I'm fine. Nothing happened.'

'You were attacked!'

'And you wrecked your scooter and injured yourself somehow! I've already told you my story. I haven't heard yours at all. All I know is that your leg is swollen and your scooter looks like it's been through a war zone.' She used her hands for emphasis. 'What ... happened?'

Baz sighed and told her the story.

'You were hit by a car! What the hell? Why didn't you go to hospital? Why didn't you call me? Why didn't you go to the police?'

Baz was indignant and possibly a bit hysterical. 'You're a cannibal!'

Daisy's jaw fell open. 'Oh gosh. I am.' She collapsed into fits of laughter, which eventually turned into tears.

Baz laid down her slightly sticky fork and placed her hand over Daisy's. 'I'm so sorry. I don't know why I said that. What came over me? I don't want to blame the hormones but I swear sometimes I just cannot control my moods. Or my mouth, apparently.'

Daisy squeezed her hand and smiled. 'We're going to be okay. We'll get through it together.'

'Always.' Baz fought back a tear. 'And we really should contact the cops about your attack last night.'

Daisy's lips twisted. 'I'm not convinced they'll do anything.

Everything I've heard says they're not taking this guy seriously. That's why we're doing these self-defence classes.'

Baz inhaled. She was about to reply when Daisy raised a hand. 'I said I'm not convinced they'll do anything – not that I wouldn't report it. I will.' She nodded for emphasis.

'Thank you.' Baz smiled. 'I'm glad. Should we call right now?'

'You're going to meet your friends soon, aren't you?' Daisy looked at her.

'Well,' Baz said. 'One of them might loan me a mobility scooter for a few days. She'll be here soon. But I'm not going anywhere if you want me to stay.'

Daisy began clearing up the breakfast dishes. 'No, it's fine. We'll call when you get back. I want some time to sit down and write up my account of what happened before I talk to anyone.'

Just then, there was a knock on the door. Daisy went to answer it.

'Oh, it's you,' said a cheerful voice. 'Where's Clockwork Orange?'

'Morning, Carole,' Baz called. 'I'm just through here.'

The hum of the scooter only just preceded Carole – and Cookie – into the room. She wheeled in at as close to a break-neck speed as the thing would go. And certainly far too fast for use inside a small inner-city flat. And yet, she wielded it like a pro, bringing it to a dead stop mere inches from Baz, leaping off with the agility of a woman half her age. Of a *gymnast* half her age.

'Thank you, Carole. I can't tell you how grateful I am. I've banged up my good leg and can barely hobble a few feet without falling down.'

Carole nodded sagely. 'The units of weights and measures in Europe are based on the German monetary system.'

Daisy looked up from where she was fussing over Cookie to give Baz a curious look. Baz tried to gesture that everything was fine. 'I hope it's not too much trouble, though. Will Peggy be all right without it for a bit, do you think? The company's sending a loaner one tomorrow afternoon.'

'Peggy's as right as rain – don't you worry,' said Carole. 'She's actually a Hittite – did you know that? She was the victim of a government plot to revive the Hittite race in order to cause congenital infertility. Of course, you know about that – don't you?'

Baz tried to prevent her mouth from opening and closing like that of a goldfish but she wasn't entirely successful. 'I'm not sure I do know about that, dear. Perhaps you can tell me while we make our way to Wellbeloved? Daisy, would you mind just helping me into the scooter and we'll get out of your hair?'

Although the last bit had clearly been addressed to Daisy, Carole responded by scooping Baz up with the strength of a tiger and the gentleness of a kitten, depositing her in the seat of the scooter before Daisy could even cross the room. 'The girl's got something in her hair, you say? Is that why it looks so sticky?'

Holding back a chuckle, Baz mouthed an apology at Daisy. Aloud, she added, 'Are you sure you'll be all right, honey? I won't stay long.'

Daisy gave Cookie a final cuddle and stood up. 'I'm fine, Nan. You go. I'm going to do my writing and I'll see you when you get back.'

'Of course,' said Carole as she led the way out of the flat, 'you know that the Hittites have been extinct for thousands of years. It was Napoleon who put a curse on them which led to their downfall. But then John Major initiated a secret plan to revive them. This was in coalition with JFK, of course, and it was all part of Charlemagne's plan to bring about congenital infertility.'

Carole prattled on like this for the whole fifteen-minute walk to Wellbeloved. It would have been quicker but, despite the rain, Cookie stopped to sniff every fence, bin, bollard, and blade of grass along the way.

Through the front window, Baz spied Madge and Peggy in their usual seats.

And it finally dawned on Baz that she wasn't going to be able to make it from the spot where she normally parked the scooter to the door and through to the second room. And the space inside was much too tight for the scooter.

It was probably a grand total of five metres' walking – but that was too much for now. 'Oh dear.'

'What's up, MacDuck?' Carole stood beneath the shop's awning and studied the windowsill. 'Park your horse. We've got a war to wend and a pageant to paint.'

Baz tried to picture what any of that sentence meant and then shook her head to clear the bizarre, jumbled image from her mind. 'Um. I'm sorry, Carole – I didn't think this through. Unfortunately, I don't think I can go inside today.'

'Well, no worries,' said Carole with her usual good cheer. She handed Baz Cookie's lead. 'Oh, by the way. Did you know King James the First wrote the computing language?' She walked into Wellbeloved, leaving Baz wondering what she was supposed to do next.

'It looks like it's just you and me for the time being, buddy,' she said to the dog.

'Woof,' said Cookie as cheerfully as Carole might have done.

What was she supposed to do now? She couldn't very well leave with Cookie but nor could she go into the café. 'Maybe if I knock on the window, Peggy will come out and collect you.'

Annoyingly, she was too far away to reach the window – and then there was the not-inconsiderable matter of the table that occupied the space between the window and her.

'Hmmm. Bear with me for a minute while I figure this out. I think I just need to...' Baz pulled the mobility scooter up the street a ways to where the pavement widened so she could get turned around.

'Oi! Where do you think you're going with my dog?'

'Morning, Peggy. Just getting myself turned around. Give me two secs.' Peggy's scooter handled very differently than the one she was used to. What should have been a simple three-point turn became a rather embarrassing eight-point turn. And one that required all her concentration – especially as she was conscious of not running over poor Cookie's toes.

When she finally managed to get herself facing the right direction, she was met with a sight that brought her to tears.

'Good heavens.' Peggy zipped her coat up. 'Pull yourself together, woman. We moved seats – we didn't burn the place down.'

Madge looked like she didn't know what to do with her hands – she must have left her knitting bag indoors. 'A little change is good for the soul.' She ran her hand along the surface of the outdoor table's glass top and scowled at her fingers. 'Sometimes.'

Sarah brought Baz and Carole's drinks out and laid them on the table. 'You look like you've been through the wars, Ms Spencer. Are you all right?'

Carole grinned. 'Well, of course, we've all been living through constant nuclear war since the government began testing back in 1872.'

Baz thanked Sarah and assured her she'd be back to normal soon. She poured herself a half cup of tea as Sarah disappeared back indoors. The brew hadn't steeped nearly long enough but Baz couldn't wait.

After taking a sip of her weak tea, Baz wiped away her tears with the back of her hand. 'I'd hate for you all to get wet on my account.'

Peggy arched an eyebrow and looked Baz in the eye while she slowly extended one finger. Her index finger, that is. Not any other finger.

Baz followed the aim of the erect digit. 'Ah. The awning.'

'Yes. The awning,' replied Peggy. 'It protects us from the rain. Gravity works the same in Canada – does it not?'

Baz smiled gratefully.

'Good,' said Peggy. 'Because I feel like four elderly women sitting around discussing the weather is simply a cliché too far.'

Madge nodded solemnly. 'Now. What's happened to you?'

Baz sagged into herself. 'Quite a lot, as it happens.'

Her friends were shocked, disgusted, and impressed at all the relevant points in her two stories. Madge insisted on checking out Baz's knee right there on the street. She pronounced Rick's handiwork with the dressing 'adequate' and repeated all the same instructions he'd given her yesterday.

When hearing how Daisy had ultimately defeated her attacker, Peggy punched her fist in the air and whooped. 'Well done, Daisy. No woman should ever be afraid to fight dirty when the situation warrants it.'

'I'm not sure she feels that way.' Baz shook her head. 'Every time she thinks of it, she gets sick.'

'Bloke was probably pumped full of growth hormones.' Carole raised her tea to her lips and took a dainty sip. 'It's how they hold the population at a mental age of three months, you know. She should get tested.' Suddenly an uncharacteristically serious look came over her. She gripped Baz's arm. 'But tell her she mustn't let them send her to a homeopathic hospital.

Those places are just a front. They'll swap her out for an impostor and you'll never get the real Daisy back.' Still not releasing Baz's arm, she added, 'Do not let that happen.'

Baz nodded. 'Thank you, Carole. I'll bear that in mind.'

'Tell her to read the book *Skating on Dry Ice*. It explains everything.' Carole touched a finger to her temple.

Laying her hand atop Carole's, Peggy looked at Carole with a warm smile Baz had never seen her bestow on anyone.

Madge crossed her arms over her bosom, still looking awkward without her knitting to occupy her lap. 'Well, I guess we've still got work to do.'

CHAPTER 13

in which a shocking revelation is made

FOR LUNCH, Carole asked Peggy to make sandwiches with cottage cheese and pickled ginger. They were odd but tasty. And, at this stage, nothing Carole said or did surprised her. That trick with the knitting needle had come close, though.

Truth be told, she hadn't been entirely surprised when Carole had killed Tom Jackson. The pair of them did have a certain degree of history. And Madge too. Though Peggy was fairly certain Baz didn't.

But the casual manner in which Carole had killed Tom had come close to surprising Peggy.

Peggy herself had only ever participated in killings that benefited society. It wasn't pleasant work, but someone had to do it. Apparently. Since the police showed no interest in removing these offenders from society.

After lunch, Carole washed the dishes and Peggy dried. Peggy was rather proud of the set they'd accumulated over the years – some antiques, a few handmade items, and some that weren't particularly unusual but were still rather nice.

As Peggy placed the plates back in the cupboard, her phone buzzed. She picked it up and looked at the screen.

BAZ

Rental scooter's arrived. I can get Daisy to bring yours back to you but not until this evening. She reported the attack and the police are sending someone over shortly to take her statement. Good grief! Remind me to tell you about the experience of calling them in the first place.

Peggy tapped out a quick reply.

PEGGY

I'll pop round now to collect it.

She'd already put her tartan coat on and grabbed her handbag when the phone buzzed with Baz's response. Chucking the device in her pocket without looking at her screen to see what it said, she kissed Carole on the cheek. 'Cookie and I will be back in an hour or two, my love.'

Carole gestured at Peggy's purse. 'You know the issue with handbags, right? If you have a clutch bag, it's meant to contain a basket of eggs. And of course a piña colada is made of pineapple and coconut and eggs.'

Peggy smiled as she and Cookie headed out the door. Carole was... Peggy wasn't sure how to finish that sentence even to herself. She was away with the fairies most of the time. And yet she wasn't. She saw everything – everything. She understood far more than most people gave her credit for. And so what if she chose to live in a fantasy world of her own creation? If she was still aware of the goings-on in this world, did it really matter that she chose not to devote all of her attention to the here and now?

One thing was undeniable: Carole was the love of her life. There was nothing Peggy wouldn't do for that woman.

Peggy leant on her cane as Cookie relieved himself on a lamppost.

Peggy's mobility had been failing her for a few years. Eventually, the stairs up to their old second-floor unit had begun to take a real toll. Thankfully, they hadn't had to look far for a new place. A ground-floor unit just behind Wellbeloved had opened up around three years ago and they'd made the move.

Once upon a time, the walk to Deptford Bridge, where Baz's building was, would have taken her a mere five minutes. These days, it took her rather a lot more than that. She scowled with each step, her hips grinding in their sockets as she moved. Still. Her mobility was better than Baz's – even when Baz's good leg wasn't banged up.

It was Madge who had first suggested the mobility scooter to Peggy. That had been two years before. They'd been friends for almost five years now, ever since ... events ... had brought them together. And those events had been necessary too. Just as Tom's unfortunate end had been.

Would this Goldsmiths Groper end in a similar way?

She shrugged to herself as she waited for the light to change at Brookmill Road.

She hadn't expected to like the mobility scooter. Madge had persuaded her to hire one for a few weeks just to get a feel for it. She'd been begrudgingly won over. As her hips had worsened, Peggy's world had grown smaller. By the time she'd finally conceded to giving the scooter a try, she hadn't been further than the Tesco at the top of the high street in a fortnight.

The first day she'd had the scooter, she'd taken Cookie for a wander. They'd soon found themselves at the waterfront, next to the *Cutty Sark* in Greenwich. She'd had to stop for a drink at the Gypsy Moth because the poor dog was too tired to go any further.

The light finally changed, giving Peggy the right of way. But, wouldn't you know it, just as happened to Baz the other day, the driver turning left cut into her right of way. Peggy thumped the car bonnet with her cane and shouted a few choice words.

Eventually, she made her way across the intersection and to Baz's building. Peggy desperately needed to sit down – not that she was going to admit any such thing to the nimble young thing working the front desk. The young man – not Jessica – called up for her and then let her through, the whole time eyeing Cookie as if the dog were about to attack.

She scowled at her reflection in the lift's mirror. Who was that old woman? Her spiky hair was blue this week. She wore a studded choker at her throat. Her trademark tartan coat was covered in pins and badges of all sorts. Ban the bomb. Never trust a Tory. She/her. A rainbow flag. Support striking workers. Refugees welcome. Don't blame me – I voted Remain. Tofu-eating wokerati. Black Lives Matter.

Last year, she'd swapped her twenty-hole Doc Martens boots for a shorter fourteen-hole pair with a sneaky zip on the side. The arthritis in her hands wasn't so bad – but she needed to save her fingers for her writing.

Although she'd never expected to grow old at all, at least she'd had the self-respect to do so disgracefully.

She exited the lift and walked the final few steps. Baz's door swung open before she'd had a chance to knock. 'Oh! Peggy, it's you,' said Daisy. 'I assumed it would be the cops.'

'Did you not get my last text?' called Baz from the living room.

Peggy strode into the flat and made straight for the sofa. 'Afternoon, Baz. My hips are killing me. Do you mind if I sit for a bit?'

Cookie was enjoying the fuss from Daisy. The two acted as if it had been years rather than hours since they'd last seen one another.

'Um.' Baz was sitting on the chair next to the sofa. She looked at Peggy like she really wanted to say no but knew that she had to say yes. Also, Peggy was already sitting. 'Sure. Of course. I can get you a tea if you'd like.'

Peggy shook her head. 'Oh, I can't abide tea. Thank you, though.' Peggy faced Daisy. 'And how are you, my dear? All recovered from your awful encounter?'

Keeping a hand on Cookie's head, Daisy looked up at Peggy. 'It wasn't that bad, honest. He gave me a good scare – left me feeling shaken up. But really, I'm fine. I fought him off. Did more damage to him than he did to me in the end.' She was putting a brave face on – presumably for Baz's sake.

When Daisy joined Peggy on the sofa, Cookie climbed up and laid his massive form across the space between them.

Peggy looked over at Baz to see if she minded Cookie covering her sofa in his hair. But she simply shrugged.

'You did well, kid.' Peggy raised her chin. She was as proud of the girl as if she were her own kin. 'And I hear you're teaching other women how to defend themselves too. You teach them all to fight dirty if they have to – just like you did. No shame in that.'

Daisy cringed. 'Nan told you about that? Ugh. I honestly feel more violated by that than anything else. I can't believe I —' She covered her mouth with her hand as though to stop herself spewing. A shiver overcame her. 'I managed to fight him off. And yet, I still feel like he violated me. You know? He interfered with my bodily autonomy. I didn't ask to swallow a piece of him. It's just so...'

Daisy bent over Cookie and buried her face in his thick fur. He was good for that.

Peggy looked at Baz and raised a questioning eyebrow. 'You've spoken to the cops, I take it? Have they been helpful?'

Daisy's eyes were red when she sat back up and she was biting her lower lip. 'They've been...' She released a noise somewhere between a laugh and a scoff. 'They're sending someone over to take my statement this afternoon. We thought they'd be here by now, actually. But the person I spoke to on the phone was...' She closed her eyes.

'They weren't very helpful,' Baz finished. 'The questions they asked her were—'

Daisy shook her head and picked the thread back up. '"Where did you first meet him? How much had you had to drink that night? What were you wearing? How far had things gone when you changed your mind?" Honestly, I'm not a violent person but I wanted to reach through the phone and grab the person by the hair and make them listen to me.'

Daisy brought her left hand to her face and pressed it to her upper lip, her face going ashen.

Peggy laid a hand on the girl's forearm. 'You are not your body. Yes, it's true, your body belongs to you and no one but you. But it is not you. Who you are is ephemeral, eternal, non-corporeal. And no one can touch you – the real you – without your express permission. Any harm he did to your physical person is ... unforgivable. But do not let him infect your soul.'

A thought occurred to Peggy and she grinned a grin that she hoped was only slightly evil. 'I remember Madge telling me something once. Now it's possible she made it up. Don't tell her I said this, but it's even possible she was just plain wrong. I'm going to tell you anyway. Maybe it will give you some comfort.'

Daisy turned herself to face Peggy, her face a picture of innocent curiosity. 'What is it?'

'When a dog bites a person, about twenty per cent of the

time the wound will become infected.' Peggy smiled once more. 'But when a human bites someone and breaks the skin, the chances of the wound becoming infected are closer to a hundred per cent.'

Daisy's face blanched.

'So, my dear,' Peggy continued. 'However miserable you may be feeling about what happened that night, rest assured that you have left that monster of a man worse off. You have done genuine harm to his physical person.' She smiled as saccharinely as she could manage. 'You won that round, kid. Never forget that.'

Daisy sniffed as she brushed a tear from a steely blue eye. 'Thanks, Peggy. That's...' She chuckled. 'Well, it's a really freaking weird way of looking at things, if I'm honest. But it does actually make me feel better. Thank you.'

Peggy crossed her arms and leant back as Daisy studied her.

'You're a bit of a freak,' the girl said eventually. 'You know that, right?'

Peggy beamed with pride. 'What? You only just noticed?' she asked at the same time as Baz exclaimed, 'Daisy! Don't be so rude.'

Peggy winked at Daisy. 'Nothing wrong with being a freak and a weirdo – am I right?'

Daisy leant closer to Peggy and whispered, 'It's okay. I'm a bit of a freak too.' Whatever else she was going to say was cut off by the trill of the entryphone. She leapt up. 'That'll be the cops this time.' She went to buzz them in, then began pacing the room. After a minute, before the officers had made it to the flat, she ran from the room. 'I'm not sure I can do this.'

Peggy heard a door somewhere in the flat slam shut just as there was a knock on the door.

Baz grimaced as she tried to get to her feet, so Peggy waved a hand in her direction. 'You sit. I'll get it.' Baz thanked her as she made her way to the door, Cookie on her heels.

She opened the door to find Madge's grandson and his obnoxiously handsome partner standing there. 'Peter. Mike. Please come in.'

Peter's face was a picture of confusion. 'Auntie? What are you doing here?'

Mike graced Peggy with an oily wink as he elbowed the young constable. 'Mrs Trent, isn't it?'

Peggy threw some ice into her voice. '*Ms* Trent.' Well, even more ice than usual, that is.

Peter swallowed. 'Sorry, yes. I mean, it's lovely to see you, Auntie.'

'Come in, come in.' Peggy motioned them into the open-plan living area. 'The elder Ms Spencer is in here. The younger Ms Spencer will join us in a moment.'

Peter slapped his hand to his head. 'Spencer!' He reached a hand out to shake Baz's. 'Sorry, I forgot your name was Spencer.'

Baz pulled herself up and out of her chair, still limping. She shook Peter's hand but her eyes were fixed on the other man. Her skin flushed and she stammered her words. 'How lovely to see you both. Thank you for coming.'

Both men wore the standard London copper uniform, complete with stab vest and hat. Mike wore a black uniform jacket over his but Peter didn't.

'Can I get you gentlemen a tea while we wait for Daisy to join us?' Baz waved in the direction of the kitchen.

Mike's dimples appeared as he held a bottle of grapefruit juice aloft. 'Thank you, ma'am. I'm fine as I am.'

Peter rolled his shirtsleeves up, revealing a neat bandage on his forearm. 'I'd love a cuppa, thank you. Black. Two sugars. Cheers.'

Peggy followed Baz to the kitchen to help with the preparations.

Mike looked up from where he and Peter were both petting Cookie. 'Now I can't promise we'll be able to get your granddaughter the justice she deserves. These muggings can be notoriously tricky to—'

Peggy coughed to cover the low growl forming in her throat. Cookie, sensing his mistress's displeasure, ran to her side.

'She wasn't *mugged*,' said both Baz and Peggy simultaneously.

Peter nodded as he rubbed his bandaged arm. 'Yes, ma'am. Sorry, I did read that in the initial report. She fought the attacker off, didn't she?'

Baz set the kettle down on the kitchen counter. 'True, she did. But it wasn't a mugging.'

Peggy slammed her cane down on the floor – the rubber tip robbing her of the solid crack she wanted. 'Rape. The word you are looking for is rape.'

Mike raised his hands in a placatory sort of gesture. 'That's a very strong word you're using. Let's have a chat and see what we can find out, shall we?'

Baz stirred the tea. 'Officer, I appreciate what you're saying. I worked with the police myself. Attempted rape can be very difficult to prove but a crime is a crime. My hope in encouraging my granddaughter to report this is that when this fiend is apprehended, her story will contribute to the larger pattern. And I also hoped that with more and more people coming forwards to report the attacks, that...'

Still stirring the same cup of tea, Baz appeared to choose her next words carefully. 'That the Met see the importance of these attacks and that they will assign the case the resourcing it so clearly requires.'

The testosterone-fuelled PC smiled smoothly. 'I understand that, ma'am.'

Gripping the counter with one hand, Baz put the other on her hip. 'Peggy, would you mind carrying the tea through to the table? Oat milk's in the fridge and sugar's up there. I'll just go see if Daisy's ready to talk.'

Peggy poured some oat milk into a small jug and pulled the sugar pot down from the cupboard. She added them and the three mugs of tea to the serving tray. Peter came over and carried everything to the table. And then the three of them stood there awkwardly as they waited for Baz and Daisy to return.

After a few minutes, a door opened somewhere and two sets of footsteps made their way down the hall.

Daisy walked in ahead of Baz; her eyes were red but she was smiling. The two officers approached her. Both reached out to shake her hand.

And that's when everything went pear-shaped.

Inches from the men, Daisy raised both her hands in the air before tripping over herself as she backed away. 'No, I'm sorry. There's been a mistake. I'm sorry you wasted your time. Please. I can't do this. Sorry to have troubled you. Thank you for coming.' She all but ran to the door of the flat. She held it between herself and the two men, like a shield.

'Er, okay?' Peter looked at Peggy as if she could explain. He grimaced slightly as he rubbed his bandaged right arm with his left.

Mike held his hand out again. 'No trouble at all, ma'am. If you change your mind, you have our number.'

Daisy slammed the door behind them, before bolting the lock and applying the chain. Peering through the peephole, she watched for a few minutes. Baz and Peggy looked at one another. Peggy blinked repeatedly. Baz made a small shrug.

After a few moments, Daisy turned around. She swallowed.

Baz limped over to her. 'What's wrong, honey? Did you get cold feet about report—'

Cupping her hand to her mouth, Daisy whispered, 'That's the man who attacked me.'

Peter's bandaged arm swam before Peggy's mind's eye.

CHAPTER 14

in which the deptford crafters' circle disbands

BAZ AWOKE to find a text from Peggy that had come in shortly after midnight. Direct, not part of the group chat.

PEGGY

> It would probably be best if you stay clear of Wellbeloved tomorrow. Possibly longer.

> You know how I feel about your Daisy. I'm not suggesting she's made this up. But, well, you must also know how protective Madge is of her people. And, to be honest, having known Peter for years, I'm not sure what to think either.

> Just give us some space to – as the kids say – process this.

Baz hurled the phone across the room. It crashed into the mirror on the back of her door, sending it tumbling to the floor, where it broke into about as many pieces as you'd expect for a full-length mirror.

Immediately, there was a thump in the room next door and

a moment later Baz's door rattled. 'Don't come in,' she shouted. 'I mean, sorry. I'm fine. Just don't come in without shoes. There's broken glass everywhere.'

Daisy's face appeared at the crack of the door but she stayed on the other side. 'Are you sure you're okay?'

Baz nodded. 'I'm fine. Some of the glass could have gone under the door, though. Be careful when you turn around. Actually, would you mind grabbing me the vacuum and a pair of shoes, please? And don't forget to put your own shoes on when you come back.'

'Sure.' Daisy disappeared.

Baz surveyed the mess without moving closer to it. She shouldn't have thrown her phone.

With her shoes on, Daisy's footsteps were even louder in the hall. Such a delicate, dainty thing in so many ways. And yet, goodness, that girl could stomp. She shouldered the door open. In one hand, she carried Baz's orthopaedic shoes; in the other, she held a small stick vacuum. 'Here you go.' She handed the shoes to Baz and set the vacuum on the floor. 'I'm just going to fetch something to put the big shards in. I'll be right back.'

She disappeared out the bedroom door – then reappeared a second later, waving her index finger at her grandmother. 'And I do not want to see you trying to bend down to pick anything up. You can do the vacuuming – I'll do the bending.' She waved her finger at herself.

Baz raised her hands in self-defence. 'Okay, fair enough. Thank you.'

At any rate, Daisy had returned before Baz even managed to get her shoes on. Daisy lifted her long, flowy skirt up and tucked it into her waistband, then squatted down to begin her task. The first thing she picked up was Baz's phone, the screen as shattered as the mirror it had collided with.

Daisy set the device on the bed and then began collecting

the mirror's remnants. 'Are you going to tell me what happened here? Or was your phone just trying to make a break for it?'

Baz inhaled and held the breath for a moment. She was going to have to tell Daisy at some point – but she needed to tread carefully. 'That officer yesterday... The one with the bandage on his forearm...'

Daisy stopped what she was doing, holding a long shard of glass like a weapon. 'What about him?'

There really wasn't any way around this, was there? She had to be honest. 'He's Madge's grandson.'

Daisy raised her hand – then stared at her reflection in the deadly looking implement she held. She lowered the hand again. 'Hang on... The bandage! Right where I bit him.'

Baz frowned. 'I know.'

'Oh, Nan. I'm so sorry. I had no idea.' After putting the shard in the metal bowl she'd brought from the kitchen, Daisy walked over to the bed and sat next to Baz. 'I guess that explains why your phone hurled itself at the wall, eh? What happens now?'

Baz put her arm around her. 'How do you mean?'

'Well, reporting a cop to the police is an uphill battle' – Daisy bit her lip – 'you know, if it's even something you want to pursue?'

Baz studied her granddaughter's face – so sweet yet strong. 'Oh, honey! No. Of course I'm not suggesting you should drop the matter.' Was that honestly what she was thinking? That a serial rapist should go free purely because of who his grandmother was? It didn't bear thinking about.

Baz used her cane to pull herself to her feet. Her left knee was still bruised but at least she could put some weight on it. She and Daisy worked together to find and remove the big chunks of glass – with Baz pointing them out and Daisy carefully plucking them up and depositing them in the bowl.

Once they'd removed the biggest shards, Baz used the vacuum to begin clearing up the rest of the mess.

Daisy touched her on the arm and spoke over the sound of the vacuum. 'I'll grab the mop and be back in a sec.'

Baz nodded. Just as she finished hoovering, Daisy returned and ran the mop around. 'I guess it's a good thing we opted for hardwood floors, eh? Imagine how much harder it would be trying to get all those tiny slivers out of carpet.'

'Definitely.' Baz headed for the en suite. 'Thanks for your help clearing this up. I'll tell you what. Give me a few minutes to get dressed. Can we talk over tea?'

'Sounds like a plan.' Daisy bent over and squinted at the floor. 'I'll finish up here and then make breakfast.'

———

'So.' Daisy laid a plate of pancakes and veggie bacon on the table and then headed back to the kitchen. 'I take it one of your friends called or texted this morning and that's what precipitated you chucking a brand new phone at a concrete wall?'

'It was a text from Peggy.' Baz finished pouring hot water into the teapot. She grabbed the oat milk from the fridge and carried both items to the table. 'It seems that – as you might expect – Madge hasn't taken the news very well and my presence at the coffee shop won't be welcome.' She checked the table to make sure they had everything they needed and then sat down.

Daisy returned with the maple syrup and took her seat. 'So ... what does that mean? You're kicked out of the group? Hang on. Does Peggy even believe me? Is the group going to disband over this?' She picked the syrup up and held it over her pancake without pouring. 'You believe me ... don't you?'

Baz helped herself to the non-dairy butter and spread it. 'Daisy! How could you even ask that?' She sliced off a bit of pancake and ate it. Chewing gave her time to compose her thoughts. 'But, well, I mean... How sure are you?' As soon as the words left her mouth, she knew she'd gone too far. But she had to ask.

Didn't she?

Daisy swallowed and Baz thought she saw a hint of a tremor in her lower lip. 'You don't believe me! Do you honestly think I would make this up? Like, maybe I just get off on accusing random men of being serial rapists.' She pushed her chair away from the table, making a horrible scraping sound against the floor. It was the sound of Baz's heart breaking.

Baz reached out a hand and touched Daisy's arm. 'I *do* believe you. It's just that eyewitness accounts are... Well, the human memory can be tricky. Every time you think through something that happened, your memory of the event changes. What we see – what we remember seeing changes over time. If you're certain Peter was the one you saw that night then I believe you. I'm just asking you how sure you are.' She knew the question wounded Daisy and she didn't want to ask – but she had to.

Daisy grabbed fistfuls of her own hair. 'That's the thing – it's what I've been trying to tell you. I didn't *see* him!'

Baz felt all the air drain out of her. 'Okay.'

'I didn't *see* him – I smelt him.' Releasing her hair, Daisy pressed her long, dextrous fingers to her temples. 'I do understand about memory. But scent memory is different. It's stronger. When I saw those officers at the end of the hall yesterday, all I was thinking was how I had to tell them everything that happened and how hard that was going to be.'

Daisy closed her eyes and rubbed small circles in her temples. 'But when I approached them, I went to shake their hands and I ... got a whiff of that scent. His scent. That same scent from the attack.'

She looked up, her eyes bloodshot. 'It was him, Nan. I swear to you. I'm not misremembering. That smell is burnt into my memory.'

'And his arm was bandaged.' Baz set her fork down.

'Right where I bit him.' Daisy nodded.

Baz laid her hand atop Daisy's. 'I believe you, honey.'

Daisy inhaled slowly. 'Thank you. So what do we do now? How do we convince the cops that one of their own is the Goldsmiths Groper? And do you think your friends will ever forgive you?'

Baz sat up straighter, angling her head downwards. 'Forgive me? Honey, I've done nothing wrong. If they'd prefer to believe comfortable lies rather than face an inconvenient truth, then... Well, I don't need friends like that.'

Swallowing another bite of pancake, Daisy frowned. 'Do you think that's what's going to happen?'

'I don't think so.' Baz pushed a piece of veggie bacon around on her plate. 'Maybe. I don't know. The ladies are struggling. Madge is hurt – maybe I really have lost her friendship. I'm not sure. As for Peggy... She's been Madge's friend a lot longer than she's been mine. But she's ... interesting. It's a lot for her to take in. To be honest, I'm not sure what to expect. Peggy said they all just need some time to work through this.'

'Sure, I get that,' Daisy said.

'And Carole...' Baz chuckled. 'Who can predict anything with Carole? But her loyalty is to Peggy. I suspect she'll do whatever Peggy decides.'

Daisy grinned the first genuine smile Baz had seen on her in a while. 'They're such a cute couple.'

'Couple?'

When Daisy looked at her like she was an idiot, Baz finally

understood. 'Ah.'

Holding her hand to her mouth to hide her chuckle, Daisy said, 'You didn't know they were a couple! You were with Baba for longer than I've been alive – and it still never occurs to you that queer people exist.'

When Baz grimaced, Daisy stopped laughing. 'I'm sorry. I shouldn't have mentioned him. It still hurts, doesn't it?'

Baz looked out the window. 'Hari's a gay man. That's how he sees himself. We still love each other – he just can't see himself being *in love* with a woman.'

Daisy put her hand on Baz's arm. 'Why does life have to be so freaking messy?'

They ate in silence.

Eventually Baz swallowed the last of her breakfast and put her fork down. 'You know that you are my priority, right? No matter what, you come first with me.'

Daisy swallowed her own mouthful and smiled. 'I know. And I'm grateful for you. For everything you've done for me. For everything you've *lost* for me. The last thing I want is for you to lose more relationships because of me.'

Baz's shoulders sagged as she deflated. 'I lost Hari because of who I am – not because of you.'

'Okay, sure,' Daisy said. 'But your relationship with my dad is as fractious as it is because of me.'

'Your father's a bigot.' Baz took a sip of her now tepid tea. 'Well, more to the point, your mother is. But your dad's a bigot by association. He doesn't have the courage to stand up to her. That's on them. Not me. Not you.'

Daisy stood up and cleared the table. 'I've got to go past the high street on my way to my lecture. Do you want me to see if I can find a place to fix your phone screen?'

Pushing her chair back from the table, Baz stood. 'It's okay. Thanks, though. I'll walk with you if that's all right?'

CHAPTER 15

wherein madge tries beer

HALF AN HOUR LATER, the two women set out: Daisy on foot and Baz on her scooter. It was raining hard but both were dressed for it. Baz had a structurally solid umbrella that covered her and most of the scooter. In her wellies and hooded raincoat, Daisy seemed to take a childlike delight in stomping through puddles.

Baz still felt a twinge of anxiety crossing the intersection where she'd come off her scooter but, thankfully, their crossing was uneventful. They made their goodbyes at the top of the high street. Baz wended her way through the open-air market until she found a phone repair place.

Having handed her phone over to the man in the kiosk, Baz spent the next half hour perusing the market. Attendance was lower than most weeks thanks to the weather, so she was able to make her way between the various stalls on her scooter without feeling like she was inconveniencing anyone.

But what was she going to do? Making friends at her age was hard. She'd picked up her entire life and moved across the world. Of course, she'd done it for Daisy, so no regrets there.

But she'd also wanted a fresh start for herself. And now here she was, just two months later needing yet another fresh start.

She paid a man for a bag of fruit and vegetables she had no idea how to cook. Hopefully Daisy would know what to do with them. She dropped the parcel into the scooter's basket – not even certain what she'd just bought.

Baz felt absolutely lost. And lonely. She wondered how long it had been since she'd dropped the phone off.

Was that Madge in the distance? Baz turned off the high street just in case, heading down a small street, the name of which she didn't know. Without her phone, she couldn't even navigate properly.

I will not burst into tears out here in public, she thought. *I won't do it.*

Baz carried on down the street and soon came to a roundabout. On the other side, there was a pub with a red London bus parked beside it. Aha! She knew where she was now. All she had to do was turn left and she'd get to the local leisure centre – and then another left to get back to the high street.

Eventually, she headed back to the phone repair kiosk. She paid for the work and collected her phone – good as new. And there were new texts. Her heart was in her throat as she clicked to see them.

PEGGY

Well, Madge is in quite a mood. She flat out asked us to leave Wellbeloved – as if Carole and I didn't own half the bloody place.

Safe to say she won't be speaking to us for a while.

I'd like to hear what Daisy had to say if she's amenable. Perhaps this evening? I'm just trying to think where we can meet. It has to be quiet enough that we can talk (that rules the Bird's Nest out), that has toilets on the main level (thus eliminating the Brookmill), that has space to park the scooters (so much for the Albert) … and, most importantly, somewhere that Madge won't be.

CAROLE

Have a little faith.

Baz disregarded Carole's non sequitur as she tapped out a quick reply.

BAZ:

Hmmm… I can't think of anywhere either. But there must be somewhere.

PEGGY

No, Carole had it right. Little Faith is our best bet. It's just off Church Street on Creekside. You know it?

Creekside?

BAZ

Is it the one with the big red bus?

PEGGY

That's the Bird's Nest. If you ever want to enjoy a local punk show, I'll take you. But it's probably not the best place for a quiet chat. Little Faith is across the street. Shall we say 9 pm?

Nine o'clock? Good grief. Baz usually started getting ready for bed at about nine.

147

BAZ

Could we make it a bit earlier? Say seven?

PEGGY

We'll see you at seven.

———

PEGGY, Carole, and Cookie made their way down Church Street. When they got to the roundabout, they stopped and waited to cross.

Except Peggy had never been very good at waiting, so she simply glared at the approaching cars until they stopped for her. The mobility scooter helped with that. Drivers might not care about pedestrians but they didn't want to hit something that could actually damage their vehicles.

Well, most of the time. Hadn't worked out that way for Baz, poor thing. But then, she didn't have Peggy's gift of the glare.

Two oncoming vehicles – a shiny new BMW and a battered old Astra – slammed to a dead stop to let them pass. The BMW driver made a very condescending 'no, after you. Please, I insist' sort of gesture. When they'd nearly reached the island, Peggy raised her right hand and extended two fingers at the driver. Prick.

Three cars coming the other way carried on through as if they had the right of way – which of course they did. According to the law, at least. At last, a white van pulled to a stop. Its driver gave a cheerful wave and let them cross. Peggy gave a curt nod in acknowledgement.

Despite the icy chill in the air, a few die-hards sat in the pub's beer garden. One of them ran over to give Cookie a cuddle as Peggy parked her scooter. Ordinarily, she was happy for him to receive his due but on this occasion it was as cold as Thatcher's heart outside and she was in a rush to get indoors. She was pleased to note Baz's scooter already parked up.

When they pushed open the door, Baz waved them over. Situated in an old warehouse building, the pub had high ceilings and a sparse interior. A few vintage prints decorated the walls. Plain wood furniture stood atop the concrete floor. But it was warm and the atmosphere was inviting.

'Evening, ladies,' Peggy said as she removed her jacket and placed it on the bench.

'Did you know,' Carole began, 'we've been at war with Denmark for thousands of years?'

'Ladies,' said Baz.

'Hi, Peggy. Hi, Carole. And you, my favourite boy.' Daisy was on the dog in an instant. For his part, Cookie rolled his massive form onto his back, demanding belly rubs. When she complied, he kicked his hind legs, shaking the closest table so violently that he almost spilt the occupants' beer. 'Sorry, sorry. I almost had to buy you guys your next round there.'

The two young lads at the next table blushed at the pretty young lady talking to them. Frankly the whole thing was far too saccharine for Peggy's liking. 'I'll go to the bar. What's everyone having?'

Baz and Daisy both gestured at their own full glasses and said they were fine for now. Leaving Cookie in Daisy's capable hands, Peggy went to the bar.

When she returned to the table, Peggy said, 'I gather your grandmother told you what this was about.'

Daisy nodded.

Peggy raised her pint to her mouth – pausing to investigate the aroma profile. Floral, citrusy, maybe a hint of pine. She took a swig. 'First of all, I want to be absolutely clear. I believe you were attacked and I am deeply sorry to make you relive that event this evening. What I wanted to discuss with you tonight is what led you to conclude it was Peter Ibeh.'

She raised a hand to pre-empt the girl's reply. 'Your grandmother loves you. That love may – not does but *may* – colour the faith she puts into your words. For my part, I like you – which is more than I can say for most people. But still, I try to be an impartial judge. So, with that in mind, please help me understand your logic in pointing the finger at a young man I know' – she raised a finger once more – 'and also like.'

Daisy's breath caught as she inhaled. She took a long swig of her own pint – a stout or porter by the look of it. After a moment, she raised her eyes to the pub's ceiling. She explained about coming down the hall, going to shake the officers' hands, and recoiling from the scent.

Peggy set her pint down. 'And there was Peter with a bandaged arm.' She didn't add that it had clearly been bothering him – almost as if it were itchy or infected.

'I had no idea who he was or that either of you knew him.' Daisy held her hand out in front of herself, fingers splayed. 'I didn't see my attacker, so I don't know what he looked like. But that smell—' She slapped her hand to her mouth. 'That smell. I will never forget that scent as long as I live. And I can't get it out of my head. That's the man who—' She looked around herself and dropped her voice. 'He's the one who tried to rape me.'

Daisy blinked. Baz put her hand on the girl's shoulder. Cookie, bless him, stood up and put his face in Daisy's lap. Her eyes glistened as she took his face in her hands.

Carole looked at Daisy and nodded solemnly. 'When I first started school in 1879, thirty per cent of the population were slaves, who were held at a mental age of three months by having their growth hormones removed. Today, that figure is ninety-seven per cent.'

Daisy cocked her head and frowned.

'Well,' said Baz. She raised her eyebrows, asking a silent question.

Peggy nodded. 'Well, indeed.' She took a long drink, draining the rest of her pint.

Daisy leapt to her feet immediately. 'I'm going to run to the washroom and then I'll get the next round. What's everyone having?'

'A pint of cider, please,' said Baz. 'Thank you, honey.'

'Shifty,' said Peggy. At Daisy's confused look, she clarified. 'Mine's a pint of Shifty, please. And Carole will have a pint of the Helles.'

As Daisy headed to the bar, Baz looked at Peggy. 'Well?' This time, it was definitely a question.

Peggy touched a finger to her lips. 'I've always liked Peter. Until tonight, I'd have sworn blind he was a good egg.' She inhaled slowly. 'But Daisy's story is a convincing one. I wish I could see a way for her to be right and him to be the person I've always believed him to be.'

Baz made a sympathetic head tilt.

'Can you believe it?' Carole said. 'They've started genetically combining the Hittites and the Mesopotamians. It was at Oxford, you know. Rather than marriage, of course.'

Peggy smiled and wrapped Carole's hand in her own.

Baz picked at a spot on the table. 'What will we do about Madge? She's not going to want to believe this.'

Peggy considered this. On the one hand, Baz wasn't wrong. Not at all. But...

A gust of frigid air slapped Peggy in the face as someone opened the door. She looked away then had to fight the urge to do a double take as her brain registered the figure who'd just entered the pub.

Madge, bundled up against the cold, approached their table

and laid her beringed hands on its surface. 'Good evening, ladies.'

Peggy looked a question at Baz, who raised an eyebrow in reply. Crossing her arms over her thin chest, Peggy said, 'Madge, why are you here?'

Madge leant back and spread her arms wide. 'Is it so far-fetched that I would simply choose to patronise this fine establishment, my dear? I have been known to enjoy a tipple of an evening – as much as anyone.'

Peggy cocked an eyebrow. 'For one thing, this is a brewery, and you, *my dear*, are not a beer drinker. For another thing, you have told me you consider this too far to walk for an evening out. And lastly' – Peggy made a show of peering around Madge to the left and then the right – 'you clearly arrived alone. And I know for a fact you consider drinking alone to be a sin. Explain yourself.'

Madge held her handbag in front of herself like a shield. 'I came to hear what the girl has to say for herself.'

'*The girl* has a name,' said Peggy – as though she herself hadn't been referring to her as the girl all evening.

On Peggy's right, Baz crossed her own arms and furrowed her brow. 'I'll not have you intimidating her.'

Madge dropped into the seat formerly occupied by the girl in question and tucked her bag beneath her chair. 'Obviously, I shan't do anything of the sort,' she said once she'd got herself settled. 'I merely wish to hear ... what happened. How she came to conclude that young Peter is the ... the one who attacked her.'

Baz nodded slowly. 'You can ask her. She'll be back in a moment. I can't promise she'll agree to talk to you. She's already had to tell the same story twice. And it was a traumatic ordeal for her. But you can ask.

Madge was bolt upright in her chair with her hands folded neatly on the table. 'Fair enough.'

Something still wasn't sitting right with Peggy. 'How did you find us anyway?'

'Carole messaged me.'

Just then, Daisy arrived back at the table with a tray full of drinks in hand. 'Sorry, there was a queue for the toilet. Oh, hi, Ms Dixon.' She swallowed. 'I, um, I didn't know you were joining us. Would you like me to get you a drink?'

Madge bristled at the use of the word Ms but all she said was, 'Thank you, dear. I will have a ... pint of beer, please.' She turned away from Daisy, clearly finished with her for the time being.

'Um.' Daisy looked left and right, like she thought she might be being set up. 'What kind?'

Madge looked back at her for a moment and nodded. 'I'm sure the house one will be fine.'

Daisy looked as confused as one might expect but she turned and headed back towards the bar.

Peggy leant over and touched the girl's sleeve, whispering her words for Daisy alone. 'Madge's arrival is as much a surprise to us as it is to you. We didn't set you up, I promise.'

Daisy nodded.

Before she removed her hand, Peggy added, 'Get her a half. Doesn't matter what. She won't drink it anyhow.'

Daisy licked her lips. 'Thanks, Peggy.'

Peggy turned back to her friends as Daisy walked to the bar.

'Oh, did I tell you,' Carole began cheerfully. 'The Oedipus myth! We finally figured out what it means. It's a coded refer-ence to John Major and' – she chuckled and elbowed Madge in the ribs – 'now I'm not suggesting Edwina Currie was his mother, you understand. But still, they were the ones who signed the declaration at Nuremberg. It's all just mad, isn't it?'

Carole prattled on like that as the rest of the group sat in awkward silence while they waited for Daisy's return. Peggy wished she'd brought her laptop so she could work on her book during lulls in conversation. When she'd last left off, Samuel Pepys was making eyes at his beloved Evie – known to the world as John Evelyn – across a crowded hall.

Fortunately, there wasn't a queue at the bar, so Daisy returned after just a couple of minutes. 'Your beer.' She set the glass down on the table and then turned to the empty table beside them and grabbed a chair.

Madge picked up the small glass of amber liquid Daisy had placed in front of her. She raised it to her face and sniffed. Then she tasted it, making a face like she'd been waterboarded with pure acetic acid. 'Delicious,' she said without a hint of irony. She set the glass back down and pushed it away from herself.

Daisy raised her eyebrows but otherwise kept her face neutral. 'So. Would someone tell me what's going on, please?'

Baz smiled at her granddaughter. 'Madge would like to hear your story, please. She just ... she wants to understand. Would you mind repeating ... what happened? First, the attack and then what happened yesterday afternoon.'

Daisy took a slow, deep breath and then downed half her pint in a single go. And then she told her story once again.

At the end of Daisy's story, Madge puckered her lips. 'Well, this has been enlightening. Thank you for sharing that with me, young lady. I'm sorry for what you went through.' She stood up, gathered her coat and things, and faced the older women at the table. 'Despite the weekend, I suggest we take tea together tomorrow at the usual time and place.'

CHAPTER 16

in which we encounter the guarding dark

THE MEETING the next morning was brief.

Baz made a point of arriving early. Once she parked her scooter, she walked to the door. Wellbeloved's official opening time was nine o'clock on Saturday – still three minutes away. But Sarah spotted her and opened the door. 'Morning, Ms Spencer. Mum's waiting for you. I expect the other two will be along any minute.' She turned to a blond man sitting at the table in the front window of the café's main room. 'Sam, do you mind me giving a hand with the sandwiches?'

'Of course.' He stood and followed her to the back room, smiling at Baz as they crossed paths.

In the side room, Baz took her usual seat.

Madge looked up from the toddler on her lap. 'Morning, Baz.' Another youngster played with a doll on the floor beside her.

Baz's stomach was dancing a ballet but she tried not to let it show on her face as she smiled. 'Good morning, Madge. And who have you got with you today?'

Madge indicated the freckle-faced child on the floor. 'That's

George. And this is Henry. They're two of my grandbabies. Sarah's boys.' The older one had Sarah's curly brown locks and the younger definitely had her eyes.

Baz smiled at the brothers. 'My, aren't you lucky – coming to work with your mum.'

George shrugged.

Since no additional conversation appeared to be forthcoming, Baz pulled her embroidery from her bag and tried to work on it. She kept stabbing herself in the finger, though.

After a few minutes, Sarah brought a tray with two teapots, cups, and a little pot of oat milk.

Baz set her handiwork aside and made to get up but Sarah touched her on the shoulder. 'We'll just add it to your bill on Monday.'

'Thank you, dear.'

Sarah nodded. 'Come on, boys. Daddy's going to take you to the park now.' Sarah and the boys left the room. Henry had his thumb in his mouth but waved his fingers at Baz as he passed. As soon as her lap was vacated, Madge picked up her knitting bag and removed her latest project.

Every time the bell above the door tinkled, Baz craned her neck to see who it was. The fifth time it happened, at seven minutes past nine, Peggy, Carole, and Cookie arrived.

Baz's heart kept climbing into her throat as she waited for the ladies to place their orders and join them. By the time they finally did, Baz's mouth was as dry as a bag of old bones – even though she'd already almost finished her entire pot of tea.

Eventually Peggy and Carole took their seats. Cookie opted to sit on Baz's feet. He leant back, his head almost upside down in Baz's lap, and gazed up at her, tongue lolling to one side. Despite herself, Baz felt the edges of her icy stress begin to thaw in Cookie's presence. But only the outer edges.

Beneath her military-style coat with its many badges, Peggy

wore a black T-shirt emblazoned with the words 'sometimes antisocial – always antifascist'. Resting her elbows on the arms of her chair, she served Madge a fierce but curious look. 'Well, don't keep us waiting.'

Madge sucked air through her teeth. 'Why shouldn't I? You kept us waiting. Clearly time is not a valuable commodity to you.'

Peggy waved a dismissive hand. 'Don't be petty. It doesn't suit you.'

Madge carried on knitting. 'Baz showed up on time.'

Peggy crossed her arms and opened her mouth to speak but Carole beat her to it. 'And of course the Etruscans had such different theories from the Patagonians regarding the nature of time. Well, you remember what happened at Windsor, don't you?'

Madge's face softened. 'I listened to what your Daisy had to say.' Leaning over her knitting, she picked up her cup of bright red herbal tea.

Baz crossed her legs. 'She's not lying.' She could feel herself perspiring.

Madge tilted her head and studied Baz for a moment. 'Oh, I know she's not lying. I could see that much for myself.'

Baz felt a weight lifted off her shoulders. 'You believe her.'

Madge raised a hand in front of herself, index finger extended. 'I didn't say that.'

Peggy released an exasperated sigh. 'Oh, for pity's sake, Madge. The girl was plainly telling the truth. She—'

'I said she wasn't lying,' Madge snapped. 'That doesn't mean that what she told us was factually correct – only that she believes it.'

Baz swallowed the last of her tea and set the cup down carefully. 'She has no reason to point the finger at Peter. They'd never even met before that day.'

Peggy shook her head. 'Don't you dare besmirch that child. She was gracious enough to walk us through the story of her traumatic event. And multiple times at that. I've always liked Peter. Believe me, I didn't want to believe her story either. But it's plainly evident that Daisy knows what she's talking about.'

'Please.' Madge set her knitting down and raised her hands in front of herself. 'I didn't say she was wrong – only that I don't know if she's right. Daisy tells a compelling story. That much is true. But I owe it to young Peter to hear him out. Maybe there's an innocent reason that will explain everything.'

Baz admired Madge's idealism. She tried to put herself in Madge's shoes. But Peggy snorted.

'I will speak to young Peter myself,' said Madge.

Baz glanced at Peggy, who gave a tiny shake of her head.

'No,' Peggy said. 'Not good enough.'

Madge's lip curled. 'I beg your pardon?'

Peggy shrugged. 'We've all got to be there. Otherwise, what guarantee do we have that you're not just going to bury this?'

Madge poured the last of her tea into her cup and drank it slowly while the others waited. When she finished, she said, 'Fine. We'll go together. Tonight. But if Daisy is right, *I* will be the one to deal with him.' Her eyes darted to Carole. 'I will do it my way. If it must be done, it will be done by my hand and no other.'

'They're out of clam chowder again,' said Carole. Her face brightened as she added, 'Joke's on them. I hate clam chowder.'

Peggy clasped Carole's hand in her own, keeping her eyes on Madge. 'That's as it should be. We know you'll do right by him. And by everyone else in the community.'

Madge nodded and something changed in the air. Baz felt she had been dismissed. Cookie must have felt it too because he stood up and started walking to the door. Baz reached out and grabbed his harness to prevent him leaving on his own.

Peggy and Carole were on their feet. Peggy bent down and picked up her as-yet-untouched espresso and downed it in one. 'Ladies.' She accepted the harness and departed with Carole on one arm and Cookie on the other.

Baz hauled herself to her feet and gathered up her stuff. 'Thank you, Madge. I understand how hard this must be for you – I really do.' Admittedly, her son wasn't a rapist – but he was an absolute bastard. Well, more of a spineless coward. But still, she tried to take responsibility for the hurt he and that harridan he married caused.

Madge looked like she was struggling to find words but, in the end, she just nodded.

———

PETER'S FLAT was the other side of the River Ravensbourne, so it made sense for the women to meet at Baz's building. She waited for them in the lobby. Jessica, the concierge on duty, kept trying to engage her in conversation. Ordinarily, Baz enjoyed exchanging pleasantries, but she was far too on edge to enjoy it this evening.

Thankfully, it wasn't long before the other three arrived. No Cookie this time. He'd been left with Emmy for the occasion.

They set out on their way. Deptford Broadway became Blackheath Hill. They walked – or rolled, in Baz and Peggy's case – past a hotel, a car mechanic, assorted houses and flats, a pet supply shop, and a building supplies merchant. The buildings represented the enormous diversity of London in visual form. There were grand but faded Georgian townhomes alongside glass and steel boxes. There were blocks of cookie-cutter flats and architectural experiments. Some of the buildings were still being constructed, others renovated, and still others in desperate need of love.

The mood was solemn as the women moved in silence – none of their usual chatter. They all knew what would probably come next. As a parent herself, Baz couldn't begin to imagine how hard this must be for Madge.

When they rounded the corner onto Lewisham Road, the eclectic mix of low- and high-budget homes and big box retail shops gave way to a series of depressingly boarded-up small businesses. Soon, though, the street widened and greenery made an appearance. Trees lined both sides of the wide road. Well, wide by London standards.

They approached a tall brown block of council flats. Once Peggy and Baz had parked their scooters, Madge punched a code into the entryphone. They waited while it rang. After a few moments, a man's voice sounded. 'Hello?'

'Peter. It's Granny. We need to talk. Let me in.'

'Er...' There was an awkward silence, during which Baz imagined Peter looking around his flat, trying to determine if it would meet Madge's cleanliness standards. 'Okay, I'll be down in a sec. We can go to—'

'No, Peter.' Madge shook her head at the phone. 'I said let me in.'

'Er, okay.' The buzzer sounded as the lock popped. Madge pulled the door open and the women entered.

Unlike Tom's building, this one had a lift. Fortunately. Peter lived on the seventh floor. They crowded into the small space, which was lined with dark faux wood panelling and covered in notices from the council. There was a faint odour – a mix of urine and commercial cleaning products. The display above the door ticked off the floors as the lift lumbered upwards.

Eventually, the door creaked open and the women emerged in a dimly lit corridor. Madge marched straight to one of the doors and knocked.

'Just a minute, Granny,' came a reply from the other side.

'Open the door, Peter.'

'Yes, ma'am.' The door swung inwards, revealing Peter. He was dressed in a blue flannel shirt over a grey T-shirt and blue jeans. 'Oh! Er... Hi, ladies.' He rubbed the back of his neck with his left hand. 'Er... Please come in.'

Madge led the way, walking past Peter into the well-lit living room. Baz wasn't sure what to expect of Peter's home ... but this wasn't it. It wasn't fashionable but it was neat and homey. And every wall was lined with bookshelves. There were floor to ceiling books – some stacked two deep.

Peter scratched his head. 'Can I, er, get you ladies some tea?'

'Tea rhymes with V and everyone knows what happened at Versailles,' said Carole cheerily.

Peter blinked rapidly. 'Is that a yes?' He stabbed his thumb back over his shoulder. 'I'll just go put the kettle on, shall I?'

As much as Baz wanted to get this whole experience over with as quickly as possible, part of her really did want a cup of tea. It would soothe her poor nerves. 'I'd like a tea, please,' she heard herself saying.

Peter headed into the kitchen. 'Ms Trent, I know how you feel about tea. Would you like a coffee? It's only instant, I'm afraid.'

Madge glared daggers at Baz, who grimaced apologetically and mouthed the words, 'I'm sorry.'

'No, thank you, Peter,' said Peggy.

'Okay, it'll just be a minute.' Peter filled the kettle and set about prepping beverages.

Why, oh why did I ask for tea?

At first Baz took this for the living room, but when she noticed there wasn't any more to the flat, she realised the futon sofa must be his bed.

As they waited, Madge made a circuit of the room,

inspecting surfaces and checking her fingers for dust. The others selected seats and made themselves as comfortable as circumstances allowed.

While the kettle was doing its thing, Peter fetched his desk chair, wheeling it over next to the sofa and urging Madge to sit on it. She checked its surface – as though she expected it to be covered in some foul substance – before sitting down.

After a few minutes, Peter returned with four mismatched mugs of tea and placed them on the coffee table. He went out to the balcony and returned with a folding lawn chair, which he perched anxiously on. 'So, ladies.' His eyes darted between each of them as he rubbed his hands together. 'What's this all about? Not that I'm not happy to see you, of course. It's just... Well, it's a bit of a surprise is all.'

Madge pulled her handbag tight to her chest. 'Peter, you remember my friend Ms Spencer, don't you?' She held out a hand towards Baz.

Peter's eyes darted from Madge to Baz and then back. 'Yeah, sure. Ms Spencer. We've met a few times.'

'And you've met her granddaughter, Daisy, I believe?'

Peter swallowed. 'Are you... You're not trying to set me up, are you?'

Baz smiled despite herself.

'No,' said Madge. 'You are no doubt aware of the sexual predator who has been prowling our streets – the one the papers are calling the Goldsmiths Groper?'

Peter scratched his ear. 'Yeah. What's this got to do with...' His eyes opened wide. 'Oh. And he attacked your granddaughter, didn't he?' He licked his lips. 'Look, I'm really sorry for what happened to her. But if she's changed her mind about reporting the attack, she'll have to call the station and report it through the proper channels. I can't do anything off the books.'

Madge sat ramrod straight. 'It's not that. It's... There has been an allegation.'

Peter leant forwards on his chair, making it squeak. 'Yeah?'

'Daisy believes it was you who attacked her,' said Madge.

Peter's hands flew to his face. 'Me? That's ... of course it's not me. You don't...' He looked around the room, studying each woman in turn. 'You lot believe her, don't you?' His eyes turned to Madge as his voice rose in pitch. 'Granny, you know I'd never do something like that. I wouldn't. How could you even think that?' He looked like he was going to be sick.

'Daisy tells quite a compelling story about what happened to her on Thursday night.' By Peggy's standards, her tone was calm. Gentle, even.

Peter got up and started pacing around the room. 'And what? She was attacked and so it must've been me? Do you even know how unreliable eyewitness accounts are? And cross-racial eye-witnesses at that. The human brain just isn't any good at recognising unfamiliar faces of a different race.'

'She didn't *see* her attacker,' Baz said. 'She ... smelt him.'

Peter stopped in his tracks and turned to face her. 'I smell like the man who attacked her? You do get how ridiculous you all sound, don't you?'

'She got away by biting her attacker.' Baz gestured at Peter. 'On the arm. You were wearing a bandage on your right arm the day you came to interview her.'

Peter grabbed his arm protectively. 'I what?'

Madge held out a hand. 'Show me your arm, Peter.'

Peter looked away as he breathed out. 'Do I have to?'

'Peter Allan Ibeh, you show me your arm right this minute.'

Scrunching his face, Peter unbuttoned his shirtsleeve and rolled it up. Peggy switched a nearby lamp on and directed the head at Peter's arm.

Madge took a firm hold of Peter's hand and... 'Peter! What on God's good earth do you call this?'

'What is it?' Peggy and Baz ran over and leant in to get a good look.

There on Peter's forearm was ... not a bite mark, but a tattoo. A black circle with five lines slashed through it.

'Answer me, Peter,' demanded Madge. 'What have you done to yourself, you stupid, stupid boy?' She thumped him on the rear end with her enormous shoulder bag.

Peter winced and looked away. 'I didn't show you because I knew you'd murder me.' He turned back and faced the women. 'Hang on. Did you say Thursday night? I had the day off. I went to see a band up at Wembley. Didn't get home until three in the morning. There's pictures all over social media if you still don't believe me.'

Madge tossed her bag on the floor and hugged Peter to within an inch of his life. 'You stupid, foolish boy. Granny loves you, you know.'

He hugged her back. 'You've got a funny way of showing it sometimes.'

Madge patted his cheek, then headed for the door. The rest of the women followed her.

Peter raised his hands out at his sides. 'What? You come here to accuse me of being a serial rapist – and then you're just going to go?'

'I'm sorry, Peter.' Baz swallowed. 'You seem a lovely young man. I'm ... glad Daisy was mistaken. I need to go and talk to her now.' She shook her head, afraid she'd start crying. 'We need to understand how she got this so wrong.'

CHAPTER 17

in which far too many cups of tea are drunk

THE WALK home was even more silent than the walk to Peter's. And it was a hostile silence this time — rather than a reverent one. When they got to Deptford Bridge station, Baz turned left to head into her building. The others carried straight on.

No one said goodbye to one another. Well, almost.

'Don't forget,' called Carole from about twenty metres down the road. 'When they tell you they need to inspect the Wi-Fi in your property, it's all part of the Home Office's ploy to revive the Hittite race. Don't let them in!'

Baz forced a smile she didn't feel and continued on her way. Jessica was still working the front door, eager to engage her in small talk, though she shut up when she saw the look on Baz's face.

The ride to the ninth floor felt interminably long. Yet, all too soon, she found herself at her own front door, knowing Daisy was on the other side.

Steeling her nerves, she turned the handle and pushed the door open. She took a deep breath and steered her scooter into the flat then parked it in its usual spot. Her heart was in her throat as she walked into the living room, where Daisy was curled up on the sofa, watching television.

'Hey, Nan. Did you have a good evening?'

A million questions ran through Baz's head but, for some reason, the one that popped out of her mouth was, 'When you say you recognised Peter's scent, what exactly did you mean?'

One look at Baz sent Daisy scrambling for the remote. She clicked the television off and ran to her grandmother, throwing her arms around her. 'What's wrong? Something's happened, hasn't it? Let me make some tea and you can tell me all about it.'

Baz allowed Daisy to steer her to the sofa. She lowered herself into her chair as Daisy filled the kettle.

Once she'd set it to boil, Daisy said, 'So tell me what happened.' She pulled the tea from the cupboard and dropped a bag in each of two mugs.

Baz leant on her elbows. 'I will. I promise. Just, please... First, can you answer my question, please? When you say you recognised Peter's scent, what exactly did you mean? What was it you smelt?' She wasn't sure why this was the most important question but her years of investigating crimes had taught her to trust her instincts.

Daisy looked up at the ceiling. She breathed deeply as though the scent still clung to the air in the flat. 'It was some sort of cologne or aftershave – something herby and woodsy – plus his own body odour and grapefruit.'

Grapefruit. Baz's heart sped up. She clutched a hand to her chest. 'Grapefruit? An artificial fruit scent?'

Daisy wrinkled her nose. 'No, like real fruit. He must've been eating it recently.'

Oh no.

'Oh, Daisy I'm so sorry.' Baz pulled herself up off her chair and headed for the door. 'Don't make my tea just yet. I've got to go back out for a bit. I'm so sorry. You were completely right. It was Peggy and me – we screwed everything up.' She pulled her coat on as she apologised over and over.

She steered the scooter out into the night and sped like the wind along Deptford Broadway. Well, like a ten-kilometre-per-hour wind at any rate. Plus, she was careful to check for oncoming traffic when crossing Brookmill Road. She did *not* have time for a traffic accident. Not tonight.

When she got to Peggy's building, she leapt off the scooter as quickly as her injured body would allow. Her right eye twitched out a staccato rhythm as she leant on the buzzer.

An unfamiliar masculine-sounding voice answered. 'Hello?'

'Sorry. Oh dear. Um, is Peggy there?'

'Peggy?' The voice sounded young and confused. 'She lives downstairs, I think.'

Baz cursed her own ineptitude. 'Oh drat. I'm so sorry.' She looked at her watch – it was after ten. 'Sorry to disturb you so late.'

'No worries, mate.'

Baz scrunched up her eyes and tried to peer at the labels on the buzzer. What number was Peggy again? She was getting herself all in a tizzy and couldn't think straight. Shaking her head, she decided to use her phone's camera to try to get a closer look at the labels. She reached for her purse – only she'd left in such a rush that she hadn't brought it.

'Oh, for heaven's sake.'

A light inside flickered and a blue-haired figure appeared. The door swung open and Peggy demanded, 'What are you making so much racket for, Baz? You're going to wake the whole neighbourhood.' Cookie wagged his tail, repeatedly thumping Peggy in the leg.

Baz brought her hand to her face. 'I'm sorry, I'm sorry. We got it all wrong. Daisy was right and we were wrong and Madge is never going to speak to us again. Well, she's certainly never going to speak to *me* again and—'

Peggy groaned. 'Come on in. Let's get you some tea and see if we can't turn those words into something vaguely cogent, shall we?' She moved aside to allow Baz in, shoving Cookie aside as well. 'And in the meantime, you can chat with Carole.'

'I'm so sorry for disturbing you.' Baz bit back tears. 'You're probably on your way to bed. I shouldn't be disturbing you.'

'I haven't been to bed before midnight since 1973.' Peggy opened the door to her flat and pointed. 'In you go. Get yourself settled. I'll put the kettle on.' She was still wearing the torn jeans and faded punk band T-shirt she had been earlier.

Cookie led Baz into the lounge. He wagged his tail so hard, he swept everything off the coffee table onto the floor.

Carole was sitting on the sofa in a bright green dinosaur onesie. The hood was pulled up such that her face appeared inside the creature's mouth. 'Oh, Baz. Good, I've been meaning to talk to you.'

Baz sat on the chair opposite the sofa. Her breath caught as she tried to suck the tears back. 'Um, have you?' She bent and began picking up the items Cookie had knocked to the floor.

Carole shook her head as though this was the most ridiculous thing she'd ever heard. 'Well, of course I have!'

Baz tried to remember the last time life had been normal. Certainly not since she left Canada. 'About what?' Cookie wandered into the kitchen.

Carole guffawed and slapped the air between them. 'Well, you recall that South Africa was destroyed in 1982.'

'Was it?'

Carole studied her. 'Was what, dear?'

It occurred to Baz that she'd forgotten to take her shoes off and she suddenly felt very rude. 'Um.' She wondered whether she should go back to the front hallway and remove them now. Or had the damage already been done?

Carole smiled. 'It's all just mad, isn't it?'

That much Baz was sure she agreed with. 'Yes, Carole, it certainly is.'

Peggy walked into the room, deftly carrying three mugs. 'Right. Tea for both of you and coffee for me.' She set the mugs on the coffee table then settled in next to Carole. 'So, Baz. What was so urgent you had to come see us straight away?'

Cookie stood in front of Baz, watching her and wagging his tail.

'Cookie, down,' ordered Peggy. The dog grumbled but lay on Baz's feet. 'Sorry, you're sitting on his chair.'

Baz smiled at Cookie, then picked up the mug and clutched it to her chest, breathing in the warmth. 'Daisy was right. It was—'

Peggy frowned. 'Look, I like Daisy. I do. And I'm sure she was telling the truth as she understands it – but she was wrong.'

'No.' Baz shook her head.

Peggy drank her entire cup of coffee in one go. 'They can't both be right. Peter or Daisy. Neither of them is *lying* – but only one can be right. Peter proved he couldn't have attacked Daisy. Ergo, Daisy must be mistaken.'

Baz set her mug down and raised her hands in front of herself. 'No, that's what I'm trying to tell you. They *can* both be right – because they both told us what happened.' Peggy opened her mouth to speak but Baz pressed on. '*We* were the ones who were wrong, Peggy. You and me.'

Peggy furrowed her brow. 'I don't see how that can be.'

Baz nodded. 'Think about it. Daisy came down the hall. She approached the officers and made to shake their hands. That's when she smelt the man who attacked her. She freaked out and chased them both out of the flat.'

Peggy's eyes were fixed. 'And then we...' She touched her fingers to her lips.

'We put the idea of Peter's bandage in her head. Yes.' With trembling hands, Baz picked up her tea again and somehow managed to drink some without spilling it all down herself. 'Tonight, I asked her what she smelt. What do you think she said?'

'I am grateful ... grapefruit,' announced Carole.

Peggy stared at Carole for a moment. 'It wasn't Peter.' Peggy closed her eyes. 'Oh dear.' She picked up her phone and stood up. Once she'd popped her headset into her ear, she tapped a few buttons.

'Yes, of course I know what time it is, Madge.' A pause. 'I'm well aware of that too. But we need to talk.' Another pause. 'No, of course it can't wait until the morning. Get your arse over here now. We'd come to you, only ... well, stairs.' Another pause. 'Okay, fine. We'll come to you. Be ready. It won't take us long. Except for the stairs.'

Arching an eyebrow, Peggy dropped the phone into her pocket. 'Let's get moving.'

Baz pulled herself to her feet then bent back down and picked up her mug. She drained the rest of her tea.

Both Carole and Cookie had got to their feet. Cookie was dancing in excited circles. Baz grabbed the mugs off the coffee table before they could fall victim to Cookie's exuberance.

Now that Carole was standing, Baz discovered her onesie had a tail with green fabric spikes. Honestly, Baz wasn't sure why she had ever expected anything different.

Peggy put Cookie's harness and lead on him. Carole stuck her feet into bright orange wellies.

The four of them set out – Carole and Cookie on foot and Peggy and Baz on their respective scooters. They walked up the little road and turned right onto Vanguard, before making a left onto the same street that Wellbeloved was on. Peggy seemed irritated by their slow progress, but Cookie was unwilling to move any quicker. 'This dog has no sense of urgency,' she grumbled the fourth time he stopped for a pee.

A man cycling the wrong way up the street passed them. 'Evening, ladies. It's a fine time for an evening constitutional,' he said – though his words were noticeably slurred.

'Oh, George,' said Carole, her green tail swaying in the breeze. 'I keep meaning to tell you... I found out what happened to your daughter Kimberley. They're holding her in Windsor as part of the programme of enforced congenital infertility. She'll be released after Whitsun – only it won't really be her.'

'Stupid bitch,' muttered the man, trying to steer his bike away from them and only barely succeeding. 'My name's Stanley and I ain't got no daughters. As you well know!'

After a short walk, they arrived at a long, yellow brick building with exterior walkways on each level. Baz looked up at it, hoping they didn't have to climb all the way up to the fourth floor.

Peggy pointed to her right. 'We'll put the scooters just there. Madge is on the first floor.'

When Baz had parked, they headed up the stairs. At least it was only one flight. She still winced with each step, though.

'Carole and I used to live upstairs from Madge,' Peggy said as they climbed. 'It was how we met.'

'I see,' Baz said through gritted teeth. It was past her bedtime and it had been a busy day. Both knees were giving her pain.

They exited the stairwell onto the first floor. Baz followed Peggy along the walkway.

Madge was waiting for them at the second door along. 'I guess you'd better come in and explain yourselves.'

She ushered them into a claustrophobic front hallway, with a small kitchen on one side, a smaller bathroom on the other and a good-sized living room straight ahead.

The large living room was crammed wall to wall with furniture, soft furnishings, knick-knacks, and children's toys. Every stick of furniture was covered with blankets or doilies. The walls were covered with an endless series of photos of varying ages: Madge's extended family by the look of it.

The largest photo showed a younger Madge surrounded by five teens and a small girl in pigtails. Baz squinted to get a closer look. *The small girl must be Sarah.* Most of the kids were Black but Baz was surprised to note that one of the teens was a fair-skinned blond girl.

Madge crossed her arms over her chest. If Baz had to guess, there was a war being waged inside her – between pride in her family and annoyance at the women. 'My children,' she said finally.

On the dining table sat a tray with a tall china teapot, teacups, a sugar bowl, a jug of milk, and a plate of biscuits – Hobnobs and Jammie Dodgers. Most of the teacups were empty but the fourth was filled with a steaming black liquid. 'Go on. Sit yourselves down and get on with your apology.'

Peggy crossed her arms over her chest. 'We haven't come to apologise.'

Baz raised a placating hand before Madge could respond. 'Yes,' she said firmly, 'we have.' She pulled a chair out and sat down. 'Madge, we *have* come to apologise. And to explain. We know who the Goldsmiths Groper is.'

Madge took a seat as well. 'I'm listening.' She picked up the teapot and poured out three cups, distributing them around the table. Placing the coffee in front of one of the remaining chairs, she added, 'Sit.'

Cookie was the first to respond to the command. He

looked up at Madge, his tail giving a hopeful little wag, clearly hoping for a treat. When none was forthcoming, he lay down dejectedly. Carole tucked her dinosaur tail beneath herself and sat. Peggy was the last to remain standing. After a moment, she sighed and pulled the final chair out.

Baz stirred some milk into her tea. 'Not only was Daisy telling the truth in everything she told us, she was also one hundred per cent factually correct.'

Madge's face hardened into a scowl. 'I thought you said you came here to apologise. Young Peter is not a—'

Baz nodded. 'We did and we will. I just wanted you to understand – the fault is ours. Mine and Peggy's. Not Daisy's.'

Madge looked sceptical. She raised her cup and drank. You could cut the silence with a knife. At length, she said, 'Explain.'

'When she went to shake the officers' hands, Daisy said she got a whiff of the man who attacked her.' Peggy uncrossed her arms. 'It was Baz and I who got fixated on Peter's bandage.'

'Idiot boy,' declared Madge, shaking her head. 'What was he thinking – desecrating his beautiful skin like that?'

Peggy rolled her eyes. 'Oh, give over. It was a tiny piece. Very subtle. Nice artwork. I must ask him where he got it done, actually.'

'But…' Baz raised a finger to draw the focus back to herself so she could prevent an off-topic row. 'There were two officers present. And if we set aside the matter of the bandage, it could as easily have been one as the other. When I got home this evening, I asked Daisy what it was she smelt. What do you think she said?'

'I don't know,' Madge said. 'But it sure as anything wasn't young Peter.'

'No.' Baz shook her head. 'It wasn't. It was grapefruit.'

Madge narrowed her eyes.

Peggy set her empty cup on the table. 'And who do we know who's always sucking at a bottle of grapefruit juice?'

Madge leant back in her chair, crossing her arms as understanding dawned on her face. She took a few slow breaths. 'That gives me an idea. I'll need a few days, though.'

CHAPTER 18

wherein a surprise tea party is held

THE SUN WAS warm on the right side of Peggy's face as the women made their way along Vanguard. Cookie had been left with Emmy from upstairs.

At the end of the road, they turned right and made their way up Friendly Street.

'Do you know,' said Baz as they made their way past a housing estate built in the seventies or eighties, 'I think I had a friend who lived around here when I was little. Ashmolean, Ashmore... No, Ashmeade Road, I think. Gosh, I haven't thought about him in years. I wonder where he is now.'

Peggy suspected it was nerves that were making Baz so chatty.

'We lived just off the high street. Our house was one of the ones the council took back in via a forced buy-back scheme. There's a big ugly council block there now.' Baz steered her scooter onto the grass verge to avoid a car encroaching onto the pavement. 'I'm still not entirely sure how you ladies obtained all the info we need.'

If they'd been still when she'd asked, Peggy would have just winked in order to avoid passing along any incriminating info. As it was, both women were facing straight ahead.

Carole replied with a long monologue about Hittites, Audrey Hepburn, genetic manipulation, nuclear testing, and the Pope controlling the population.

When Carole paused for a breath, Madge implied that she'd used sex to obtain the info. She was probably kidding – but you could never be certain with Madge.

In truth, the women each had their sources and they never shared details with one another.

Eventually, the group arrived at an ordinary Victorian terraced house. It had an unassuming black door, dirty brown bricks, and a small paved front garden – just enough room for the bins and a couple of pot plants.

Peggy and Baz parked their scooters on the street. Once Peggy had removed a carefully packaged parcel from her basket, the four approached the door. Madge knocked.

Mike wasn't due to go on shift until the following day. Their research had left them reasonably confident he'd be home and awake this afternoon – but for a moment, Peggy thought they might have been led astray.

Just as they were about to give up and resort to plan B, Peggy heard movement on the other side of the door. Then came the sound of multiple locks being undone. He greeted them with that same ingratiatingly flirtatious smile he always did – plus a bit of confusion. 'Ladies. To what do I owe this honour?'

The others may have struggled to maintain their friendly façades. But since Peggy had always responded to him with disgust, she saw no reason to change tack now.

'We like to think of ourselves as the welcoming committee

for the neighbourhood,' said Madge, returning an equally flirtatious grin. 'We brought cupcakes.'

My gosh, it's all so vapid. Peggy was sure she could feel her brain cells dying just listening to this.

'I'm not new to the area, though,' Mike replied with a tilt of his head. 'I grew up here. Right in this very house in fact.'

'Oh, really?' Baz asked – as though they hadn't known this fact in advance. 'We thought you'd only recently moved here. Didn't you transfer from Hammersmith nick?'

The horrid man crossed his arms over his chest and leant casually on the doorframe. 'You've done your homework.' He had the audacity to wink at Baz. 'Come on in. Let me put the kettle on.'

'Oh, how thoughtful. Only if you're sure it's no trouble,' said Madge as she elbowed her way past him into the front hall.

Baz and Madge removed their shoes before heading deeper into the house.

Carole shook Mike's hand, taking his right in both of hers. He winced ever so slightly when she gripped his forearm in her left hand. 'Young man, do you know about the nuclear testing over in Windsor?'

Mike smiled at her. 'No, I'm afraid I don't, Mrs Ballard.'

Carole scoffed but maintained eye contact. 'Well, of course you don't. You with your subnormal intellect.'

Peggy chuckled like this was all some grand joke. 'Come on, dear. Give the man his hand back.' Carole finally released Mike from the handshake.

With a wink to Peggy, he said, 'Quite the grip your friend's got there.'

Peggy put her arm around Carole. 'Partner.'

Mike leant forwards. 'Pardon?'

Peggy did her best to keep her voice sweet. Well, as sweet

as her voice ever got. 'You said *friend*. Carole's my partner. We've been together almost twenty years.'

'Ah. How very modern.'

The house followed a typical Victorian layout – though it had clearly been gutted and subjected to extensive renovations. The wall between the living and dining rooms had been knocked through, creating a light-filled open-plan space. The whole thing was sleek and ultra-modern – entirely out of keeping with the spirit of the place. Peggy did not approve. Juxtaposition was one thing – but to completely steamroller the vibe of the place was unforgivable.

The officer rubbed his hands together. 'Is tea all right for everyone?'

Peggy didn't want to drink anything the man had to offer – but they had appearances to maintain. At least for now. 'Coffee for me, please. If you've got it.'

'Your wish is my command.' The prick actually bowed. The others all assented to tea. 'Here, let me take that from you. Cake, you say? I'll plate it up.' He reached for the bag in Peggy's hands.

Madge took the bundle from Peggy. 'I'll let you make the tea while I deal with this.'

He studied Madge and, for a moment, Peggy worried he was onto them. But then he shrugged. 'Fair enough. I suppose I could do with the extra pair of hands. It's not often I'm entertaining four beautiful women at once.'

Peggy resisted the urge to vomit. Carole opened her large handbag and began digging around in it.

Their voices faded as they walked through to the kitchen. Peggy gave Baz a look that she hoped the other woman understood to mean 'stick with the plan'. Baz nodded.

'Did you know,' Carole said, appearing to address a house-plant, 'the waste water from urban laundromats is fed into the domestic water supply. It's all just mad, isn't it?' She leant towards it, smiling. After a moment, she laughed. 'Yes, well, you would say that.'

Peggy wandered towards the front window. A bookshelf stood to one side of it. She always liked to see what books people had on display – their choices said so much about who they were. What would this man choose to present for his visitors?

To the left of the telly, she found several books on body language, neuro-linguistic programming, and alpha males.

A soft chuckle captured her attention. She fixed Baz with a look, a questioning eyebrow raised.

'You sounded like Madge just then,' Baz said softly.

'What?'

'You did that tongue thing,' Baz said.

Peggy furrowed her brow. 'I did no such thing.'

Before Baz could reply, Madge and Mike returned from the kitchen. He carried four matching mugs and she followed with a tray bearing five plates, each with a cupcake ensconced in a different coloured paper.

Mike put the tea on the coffee table towards the front of the house. 'Go ahead and set those down on the table, Mrs Dixon. I'll be right back with the rest. Ladies, sit wherever you like. Please go ahead and make yourselves comfortable.'

'Thank you, dear.' Madge distributed the cakes.

Peggy steered Carole towards the sofa by the front window. Peggy gestured for Baz to sit on one of the two chairs facing them. When she'd finished serving up the cakes, Madge sat on Carole's left.

A few seconds later, Mike re-emerged from the kitchen, carrying a jug of milk, a sugar bowl, and another mug.

Mike passed a mug of strong black coffee to Peggy. 'Madge says espresso is your drink of choice. I made it long – hope it's to your liking.' Peggy breathed in the aromas wafting up from her cup and almost changed her mind about the man. Then she remembered who he was.

Madge gestured at the cupcakes. 'I made these myself.'

'Thank you very much.' Mike sat down and picked up the plate in front of him. He studied it for a moment. 'That's not...' He sniffed it and smiled appreciatively. 'Is this hummingbird cake?'

Madge nodded. 'It is.'

'My favourite. You really have done your homework!'

'Young Peter might have let slip.' Madge beamed with obvious pride.

Mike tore a tiny piece from the neatly decorated cupcake and placed it in his mouth. He closed his eyes. 'Oh, wow. That is delicious. I'll have to have you ladies around more often. Maybe I'll even invite you next time.' He winked at Madge, who smiled back.

He ate a few more bites of the cake. 'So, ladies. Why have you really come? Is this about your granddaughter, Mrs ... Spencer, wasn't it? How's she doing?'

Peggy spied a tiny muscle twitching on Baz's face but she held strong. 'Daisy's doing fine, thank you.'

Mike steepled his fingers as he nodded. 'I'm glad to hear it. She learnt a hard lesson that night, I suppose.'

Baz held herself rigidly still – but she smiled and played along. 'Sorry. I'm not sure I follow. What lesson is that?'

'Oh, you know what these modern girls are like. Drinking and carousing and all sorts.' Mike raised his hands and flashed that million-pound smile of his. 'I've always been partial to older women myself.'

Afraid Baz would be tempted to strangle the young officer with her bare hands, Peggy took control of the conversation. 'Now, now. You're getting us all distracted, you naughty boy.'

She shook her index finger in what she hoped would pass for a flirtatious manner. 'We're here to learn about you. To welcome you into our community and help you understand ... how things are done in Deptford.'

'Oh, yes.' Madge leant forwards on the sofa. 'You told us you grew up here. Yet our sources tell us you're new to the area. Care to let us in on the secret?'

'It's no secret. Not really. The rumour mill doesn't have it entirely wrong.' He leant back in his chair and placed his right foot on his left knee – the picture of a man at ease. 'I moved back here from west London about four months back – but my transfer only came through last month. I've lived out Hammersmith way for most of my adult life. But I really did grow up here. My mother was' – Peggy thought she spied the slightest hint of a snarl – 'not fit to be a parent. I was placed with my grandparents when I was four. In this very house.'

Having hit on his favourite subject – himself – there was no shutting him up now. 'My grandmother was wonderful to me. She was the very best person. But she fell ill and died not long after I came to stay. So, it was my grandfather who raised me. I went to school just up the road.' He waved an arm vaguely westwards.

'And now you're back,' said Baz.

Mike frowned as he nodded. 'My grandfather died just after Christmas. As the only surviving family member, I inherited this lovely house. Though... It wasn't quite so lovely when I first got my hands on it. But I've got it looking just the way I want it now.' He was actually proud of this chrome and glass space – this magnolia and taupe room, with its bland art and its complete dearth of personality. Style without substance.

Madge sucked her teeth. 'A man like you shouldn't be single. You need a woman in your life. How is it you're not married?' By pretending she knew nothing about him, she was skilfully drawing out the bits they didn't know – filling in the blanks. And, naturally, she was keeping him talking.

Mike tossed the last of his cupcake into his mouth. Covering his mouth, he said, 'This is so good – I'll have to spend some extra time in the gym, working the calories off.' He swallowed before continuing. 'And in answer to your question … I was. Well, technically, I still am – for now. Didn't work out.'

He shrugged but something about the movement struck Peggy as forced. He was trying to make light of the situation.

'Oh, Mike. I'm so sorry to hear that.' Madge was on the edge of her seat, looking like a concerned mother. 'So, moving back here was your fresh start – your clean slate, as it were.'

That got him talking again. Eventually, he went to take another sip of his tea only to find the cup empty. 'Oh my. I should get us some more tea.'

Madge pushed herself to her feet and studied him. 'No, it's fine. I'll get the tea.'

He closed his eyes as he nodded. 'It's my house. I should make the tea.'

'We'll do it together, shall we?'

The pair of them wandered off to the kitchen. Baz swallowed as she followed them with her eyes.

'Baz,' Peggy said softly. 'Keep your nerve. Everything's going to be fine.'

Peggy held her hand out, palm upwards, and raised it slowly as she inhaled. She held the breath for a four count and then exhaled, watching Baz mirror her. Held the breath for another four count and then repeated the exercise.

Madge and Mike returned from the kitchen – she carried three mugs and he had a mug and a glass of pink juice.

When the drinks had been distributed and everyone was sitting, Peggy looked at Mike. 'I expect it was the failure of your marriage that was the trigger.'

He narrowed his eyes at her, then shook his head. 'Trigger? What do you mean? Trigger for what?'

Peggy had a talent for making people uncomfortable with her looks. 'Well, there had to be something. I'm assuming you didn't just wake up one day and decide to become a serial rapist.'

CHAPTER 19

in which plans bear fruit

THE MUSCLES in Mike's neck stood out in stark relief as he leant forwards in his chair. He blinked. 'What did you say to me?'

'We know, Mike,' said Baz softly. Her heart was like a hummingbird in her chest, fluttering away faster than she could count.

He got up out of his chair and hovered over Baz, menacingly. 'Oh really? And what exactly is it you think you know?'

Madge took a sip of her tea. 'Mmm, delicious.' She set the cup on the table. 'We know you're the one the papers have been calling the Goldsmiths Groper.'

Peggy's lips curled into something of a snarl. 'Which is a ridiculously underblown metaphor. You're a brute, a rapist, and a monster.'

Mike ignored Peggy and faced Baz, his posture relaxed. He smiled at her, dimples flashing. 'What are you – the Tuesday murder club? The Misses Marple? You fancy yourselves amateur sleuths – is that it?'

Peggy snort-laughed, her little mug wobbling in her hand.

He put his hands on his hips and took a step towards Peggy. 'Which one of you's recording the conversation? Is it you?' He side-stepped and faced Carole. 'Or maybe you – after all, no one's going to suspect the dotty one.'

He took another step and turned so he was facing Baz. 'I assume that's your plan, yeah? You'll accuse me, confront me with a bit of circumstantial evidence or maybe a bit of hearsay, and then I'm supposed to break down in tears and confess everything? That's how you thought this was going to go, right? So, come on, lay it on me. What's your evidence?' His breath was hot on her face, smelling of pineapple and grapefruit.

Baz swallowed. Without taking her eyes from Mike's, she tried to steady her breathing.

He took a noisy breath. 'This is the real world, not an Agatha Christie novel. Major crimes are not solved by little old ladies with a fetish for meddling. The police do that. And you' – he spun around the room so he could cover them all with his wagging finger – 'none of you are cops. Not even you, *Ms* Spencer. I know you used to be a strawberry.'

At Baz's puzzled look, he added, 'A civilian investigator? Oh, yeah, guess what. I looked you lot up too. I know you fancy yourselves, like, Deptford's guardian angels or something. But you're playing in the big boys' playpen now.'

Putting a hand on the back of the chair he'd only recently abandoned, he stared at Baz. 'This little joke isn't funny anymore, ladies. Leave my house now and this doesn't have to go any further. We'll all forget this afternoon ever happened. Go on.'

Remaining seated, Baz crossed her arms. 'I don't think so.'

He seemed to decide to give the good cop routine one final go, turning to Madge with that greasy smile. 'Come on, ladies. We've had a nice little chat and now it's time for you to go home. I really don't want to get the police involved but I will if I have to.' He reached into his pocket.

'I assume you're looking for your phone,' Baz said, 'so you can show us you really mean it about calling the police.'

'Filth,' said Carole.

He turned to face Carole, his eyes narrowed. His breathing was shallow.

'We removed that when we first arrived.' Peggy smiled. 'And your watch, too, of course. Carole might be a bit eccentric – but she does have her skills.'

His skin blanched as he turned back to Peggy. All that turning must have been making him dizzy. 'This is a very dangerous game you are playing. And I will ask you one last time – please leave my house. I will not ask nicely again.'

The women remained seated, silently calling his bluff.

He looked at them all, his lips almost bluish. 'I will call the police.'

Baz chuckled. 'No, you won't.'

He leant on the chair once again. 'And why, pray tell, is that?'

'Well, for one thing, as we've already discussed, we have your phone.' She cocked an eyebrow. 'And for another thing, we all know you don't want them to hear our story.'

'Zat all you got?'

'No,' said Madge. 'It's not.'

'We know, for example,' said Peggy, 'that the crimes began four months ago – coinciding with when you moved to our community and shortly after your marriage ended.'

Mike dropped heavily into the chair and leant forwards, resting his arm on his knee and using it to support his head – the picture of a man fascinated by a compelling story.

'We know that the man who attacked Daisy was drinking grapefruit juice.' Baz waved at the half-drunk glass on the table next to Mike. 'And we know that she bit her attacker on his right arm.'

His face was shiny and pale. 'You want to see my arm?'

Peggy gave him an icy smile. 'Carole gave your arm a quick, friendly squeeze when we first arrived. I saw you flinch.'

Mike nodded, his movement languid. 'Basically, you've got nothing.' A shudder went through him.

'What we've got, Officer,' said Madge, practically spitting the title, 'is a community that's about to become a whole lot safer.'

'You can put your little recorders away.' He made to stand back up again but seemed to rethink it. 'I'm not going to confess to anything.'

Baz leant forwards. 'You're not very clever, are you? You still think we came here to get you to confess. That our ultimate aim is to turn you in to your fellow officers.' She cracked a grin, though her mind was screaming *danger* at her.

Mike hurled himself off the chair and flew at Baz, grabbing her by the throat, cutting off her air supply. The world began to grey out, dimming from the edges inwards.

'Don't do it,' she croaked.

'Oh, you're going to have to do better than that if you want me not to hurt you. I want to hear you beg. Do you know how badly I've wanted to—'

Pulling at his hands, Baz managed to squeak out, 'I wasn't talking to you.'

And then Carole had him in a headlock, her knitting needle poised for the money shot. But still he didn't let go of Baz.

'Don't,' repeated Baz, looking directly at Carole. 'Not this time. You'll spoil all our careful planning.'

Not every situation could be solved by Carole and her knitting needles. The women had been able to make Tom's body disappear. There was no one to miss him, so a quick rumour about him moving to France was all it took. But Mike was a cop. If he vanished, there'd be a manhunt. If he were murdered, there'd be a nationwide search for his killers.

No, they couldn't afford to let Carole dispatch her own special brand of justice in this case. Madge's plan would ensure there were no loose ends.

Baz saw Mike's cheeks puff out. Diving across the room into Madge's lap, she managed to avoid the worst of the spray – but it wasn't very dignified. The chair where she'd just been sitting was covered in chunks of tea, cake, and digestive juices.

Pushing herself into a sitting position, Baz motioned to Carole. 'I'm all right. Deposit him in his chair, please.'

'What've you done to me?' A trail of sick slid down his chin and dripped onto his shirt.

Carole smiled as she re-sheathed her needle. 'Die, little piggy, die.'

Rather unsurprisingly, Carole's words had an effect on the man – and not the desired one. 'You think you can take me? You?' He cackled – a wet, gurgling noise – and pulled himself free of her grasp. 'You're nothing but a bunch of little old ladies.'

Peggy spoke for the first time in a while. 'I think that's rather the point, you see.'

Madge nodded approvingly. 'When the police refuse to act, sometimes we have to take matters into our own hands to ensure the safety of our community.'

'But only when strictly necessary,' added Baz. That part was important. She understood that now.

By this point, Mike was thrashing and flailing in his chair.

Baz now moved towards him. 'We need to get him under control. It can't look like there was a struggle in here.'

'Gloves, please.' Madge waved her purple disposable nitrile gloves in the air. The other women pulled their own gloves from their pockets. 'We came for a friendly chat, so our finger-prints will be here – but we mustn't leave any indication we were here during his overdose.'

Mike roared like a dying animal – which is what he was. 'What'd you do?'

Carole and Peggy managed to get him from behind. Peggy wrestled him back into his chair. Carole sat on his lap to prevent him moving. There wasn't much fight left in him, but he was giving it all he had, battering the air – not to mention Carole.

'Fentanyl,' said Madge. 'Surprisingly little of it, actually. In the cupcake. It's all that grapefruit juice you drink, you see. It interacts with it terribly – increases the potency of the drug exponentially.'

'You'll never get away with this.' His words were slurred now – barely comprehensible.

'Hold his arm steady, please, Baz.' Madge pulled a small phial and syringe from her handbag. Baz extended Mike's arm, keeping a firm grip on his wrist. 'Just one final confirmation.' She carefully rolled his shirtsleeve up and peeled the bandage away.

All the women peered at his exposed forearm. Sure enough, right where they knew it would be, there was a badly infected wound.

Madge shook her head. 'Hmm.' She affixed the syringe to the phial and called up the required amount of fluid.

'Hang on,' said Peggy irritably. 'Let me do my part first.' She fetched Carole's bag and retrieved the man's phone. Holding it up to his face, she unlocked it. 'Thank you.'

Beneath Carole's weight, the man still struggled – but weakly. The terror in his eyes was real, though. Baz supposed they'd have to live with that. It was only fair.

'I was only getting it prepped.' Madge raised an eyebrow at Peggy. 'Am I good to go now?'

Peggy was scrolling through his phone, tapping and clicking away. 'Let me just make sure I don't need his face again to access his email. There we go.'

Madge nodded and took Mike's arm in hers. 'Thank you, Peggy.' He tried to pull his arm away but Baz's grip was too strong – or maybe he simply had too little strength left. 'Farewell, PC West. I wish I could say it was nice knowing you.' She plunged the needle home.

Peggy scoffed. 'If it were nice knowing him, we'd hardly be here, would we?'

PC Mike West gave a shudder and then stilled for a final time. The late PC Mike West.

'All right, ladies.' Baz put her hands on her hips. 'We've got our work cut out for us now. Everyone knows what they're responsible for, yes?'

'We know.' Madge checked his pulse, then pulled a stethoscope from her bag. She leant over his chest and listened. She nodded. 'All clear.'

Peggy sat down with his phone and got to work. Baz took the needle from Madge and pressed it into Mike's hand, then dropped it onto the floor next to the chair.

Not quite twenty minutes later, the women headed home. She couldn't say what the others were feeling, but Baz had made her peace with what they'd had to do to make London's streets that little bit safer. She wasn't sure that knowledge would be enough to let her sleep that night, though.

CHAPTER 20

in which normalcy resumes

BAZ PARKED her mobility scooter on the little strip of pavement between Wellbeloved's outside seating area and the car park next door. It was a beautiful October day, the sun shining brightly over south-east London. She walked the few steps towards the door of the coffee shop but paused outside the beautiful old building.

It had been a month since she'd first befriended the ladies of the Deptford Crafters' Circle. So much had changed in just one month.

Daisy stood by the door, waiting for her. 'Is everything all right, Nan?'

Baz pursed her lips, ever-so-slightly smearing her rose-coloured lipstick. 'Everything's fine, honey. Just got lost in my own head for a sec.' She waved at her friends, who were sitting inside. Adjusting her shoulder bag, she took one last deep breath as Daisy pushed open the door of the coffee shop.

Behind the counter, Olena looked up and smiled. 'Good morning, ladies. You're having your usual orders, yes?'

Baz nodded. 'Yes, please, Olena.'

'Same,' said Daisy. 'But would you mind waiting a few minutes before you make mine?'

'No worries. Just let me know when you're ready.' Olena rang up the order, then nodded to Baz. 'I'll bring yours through in a few minutes.'

'Thank you.' Baz tapped her phone to the device to complete the payment.

The two women ducked through to the other room, where Baz's friends were sitting. When Cookie spied Daisy, he leapt up with an excited yip – much to the surprise of the people at the next table over.

'Oh my days! There's a dog there,' said one young man to his friend.

Everyone greeted everyone else as Baz took her usual seat.

Daisy had a whispered conversation with Peggy, who nodded. Beaming, the girl picked up Cookie's lead. 'We'll be back in a bit. Just going to the park.' The dog trotted off happily after her. She waved again as they walked past the front window.

Olena appeared, bearing a tray with Baz's tea. 'Here you go.' She set everything out on the table, then looked around the group. 'Anyone else need anything while I'm here?'

The ladies shook their heads. 'Thank you, Olena,' said Baz.

As Olena returned to the other room, the chime above the door sounded. Peter walked in with another officer, a tall blond. Both of them were in uniform. 'Morning, Granny. Aunties. This is Sergeant Piwowarska. Sarge, this is my granny, Mrs Dixon. And these are her friends, Ms Trent, Mrs Ballard, and Ms Spencer.'

The other officer nodded at the women. 'Ladies, Peter suggested we might find you here. We need to have a brief word with you. Would now be a convenient time?'

Baz swallowed her fear. 'What's this about, Officer?'

The sergeant pulled a notepad and pen from one of her many pockets. 'Just a quick chat. We can do it now – or we can arrange to come to your homes at a later time if you'd rather. But if we do it here, we can get it all over with in one go. More efficient for everyone this way, yes?'

Baz allowed herself to relax a smidge. If they were being treated as suspects, things would be going very differently.

Carole looked up at the officers for the first time since they'd arrived. 'Do you even know what the French connection is?'

Peter must have briefed the sergeant on Carole's non sequiturs, because she didn't bat an eye. 'So, what do you say, ladies, do you have time to answer a few questions?'

Madge nodded imperiously. 'Always happy to help an officer of the law. What would you like to talk to us about? And would you care for a coffee? I can have Olena bring you one.'

'Thank you. And no, no coffee for me just yet, thanks.' Both officers dragged chairs across the room and sat down with them, close enough so they could speak softly. And close enough that Baz could see how tired they both were.

'Where's that handsome partner of yours, Peter?' How Madge kept a straight face, Baz would never know.

Peter ran a hand over his tight black curls. 'Er, right. So, well…'

Peggy peered over her laptop and Madge set her knitting on her lap.

'What Peter is trying to say,' said Sergeant Piwowarska, 'is that PC Mike West is… I'm sorry. There's no easy way to say this. He's dead. Took his own life.'

Peggy clutched her chest and Madge raised her eyebrows. Without looking up from her crocheting, Carole said, 'This little piggy went to market.'

For her part, Baz composed her features. 'Oh, my gosh. We

only saw him the other day – he seemed fine. I'm so sorry for your loss – both of you. What a terrible tragedy. What happened? If you can say, that is.'

Peter rubbed the back of his head with his left hand.

'As I'm sure you can understand,' said the sergeant, 'there's a lot we can't tell you. But – and this is the reason we're here now – a few hours before he overdosed, one of the neighbours spotted four women entering his house. Based on the descriptions, we believe you were those women.'

'This would have been the day before yesterday,' added Peter.

Madge nodded. 'Yes, we paid a visit to the handsome young man on Tuesday. We had tea with him.'

The sergeant wrote something in her notepad. 'And what time was this?'

'Well,' said Baz. 'We set out around – what would it have been? About two o'clock, would you say, ladies?'

Madge touched a finger to her lips. 'Yes, I had been doing an English class. I volunteer at the local church, you see. I'm sure you're aware of the many newcomers to the UK we have in Lewisham. There's a great need for English classes – especially free ones. The lesson ended at one o'clock. I concur with Ms Spencer – it must have been about two that we met up.'

'It took us around a quarter of an hour to get there,' said Peggy. 'Baz and I could have made the journey quicker in our scooters, of course. But Madge and Carole were on foot. And Madge does *not* rush.'

The sergeant scribbled in her notebook some more. 'I see. And what sort of mood was PC West in when you spoke with him?'

'Oh, he was in excellent spirits.' Madge resumed her knitting. 'Very charming and pleasant.'

'Except...' said Baz, as they'd agreed ahead of time. 'Near the end of our visit...'

'Oh, yes,' said Peggy – as though it had only just occurred to her. 'We spoke about the safety of the neighbourhood. That was why we went to see him, really. We take an interest in the local community and we like to get to know the people whose job it is to keep everyone safe. Anyhow, we got to talking about the attacks on young women – this so-called Goldsmiths Groper. After that, he seemed to become...' She tapped her lip.

Madge picked up the thread. 'Mmm hmm. His mood definitely changed at that point. I noticed it too. It seemed to bring him a great deal of sadness. Probably because he had failed to catch the man.'

Sergeant Piwowarska looked up from her notebook. 'And what did he say to you about the Goldsmiths Groper? Anything specific you can recall?'

Baz shook her head slowly. 'No. We were the ones who mentioned it.'

Madge picked up her cup. 'I've been in Deptford since 1958. That's when my family moved to the UK from Jamaica, you see. And so I take a keen interest in what goes on in this area, as do my friends. We told young Mike our concerns for the safety of the women in Deptford and New Cross.' She took a sip of the tea.

'After that, he seemed to become' – Peggy bobbed her head – 'taciturn.'

'Perhaps,' said Baz, 'he felt the Met's inability to deal with the problem reflected badly on him.' It was a line they'd agreed on in advance. Baz worried she wasn't enough of an actor to carry it off.

But the sergeant nodded and noted it down in her little book. 'And the purpose of your visit was to discuss, how did you phrase it' – she studied her notebook for a few seconds – 'the safety of the community?'

'Mmm hmm.' Madge looked at the sergeant over the top of her reading glasses. 'We're very invested in everything that goes on around here.'

'I see. So should I be expecting you to pop around my place unannounced one day?' The sergeant smiled. 'Or is it only handsome young men who get such treatment?'

Peggy smirked. 'Oh, I don't like men.'

'I see.' The sergeant clicked her pen closed. 'Thank you, ladies. I think we've got everything we need for today. Unless there's anything you wanted to discuss?'

Baz had to bite her lip to prevent her sigh of relief from being obvious enough for the people in the next borough over to spot it. 'Thank you, Sergeant. And we really are sorry for your loss.'

Madge sucked her teeth. 'Such a shame. So sad to see a handsome young man lost from the world. And so charming, too.'

It was the sergeant's turn for a tight-lipped 'mmm hmm'. She stood, then nodded to each of the women, before returning her chair to the table she'd borrowed it from. 'Thank you for your time, ladies.'

Peter followed the sergeant's example. 'See you at lunch on Sunday, Granny. Bye, Aunties.'

Before they could leave, Daisy and Cookie returned. 'Hey. Oh, sorry. Hope I'm not interrupting.' Daisy's eyes landed on Peter. She cast her eyes down as a pink hue rose through her neck and up to her face.

'Hi.' Peter's eyes twinkled. 'It's Daisy, right? I'm glad you're feeling better.'

Cookie allowed Sergeant Piwowarska to make a fuss over him for a few seconds and then crawled under the table to get to Peggy. Walking around the table seemed like it would have been the simpler option – but try explaining that to this mountain of a dog.

Daisy looked at the floor. 'I am. Thanks. And, erm... I'm really sorry about ... you know, about before.'

The sergeant brushed her hands down the length of her uniform. 'Come on, Peter. I could murder a coffee.' The pair of them ducked through to the café's main room. Instead of leaving, they turned right, towards the coffee bar.

Daisy grabbed a chair and dropped into it. She remained silent until Peter and the sergeant left the shop a few minutes later, coffees in hand. 'So, um. I didn't want to say anything while the cops were still here. But you would not believe what a font of gossip that dog park is! If you ever want to know anything about what's happening in the neighbourhood, trust me, just ask the dog park crew. Apparently, they even have a group WhatsApp and they're forever—'

Peggy opened her laptop and started typing again. 'Get to the point, young lady.'

Daisy grinned and waved dismissively. 'Oh yeah. So one of the houses near the park is all cordoned off with police tape. And the rumour is – you are not going to believe this—'

'We certainly won't believe it if you never get to the punchline,' said Peggy.

'The house with all the activity belongs to one of the local cops. You know, one of the two who came to our place a few days ago. Not the one who was here just now – the other one. He was found dead in his house yesterday.'

'Mmm hmm.' Madge's knitting needles clacked away. 'The police just told us that.'

Daisy waved a hand for emphasis. 'Yeah, well I bet they didn't tell you this part. Turns out he was the Goldsmiths Groper – just like I said.'

The older women looked up from their crafts. Peggy raised an eyebrow. 'Really? Is that right?'

'Oh my.' Baz reached out and took her granddaughter's hand.

Daisy let out a breath. 'I know, I know. A man is dead and I'm trying really hard to care about that. But he was a...' She dropped her voice to a whisper 'He was a rapist. He attacked me and loads of other women and girls and femme-presenting people. And I just...' She shook her head. 'I find it really hard to be sad about it.'

Daisy frowned. 'Does that make me a bad person?'

Baz squeezed the hand in hers. 'No, honey. It makes you human.'

Taking a deep breath, Daisy stood up. She picked her backpack up off the floor. 'Right. I've got a class to get to. I'll see you all later. Thanks for letting me walk Cookie.'

Peggy nodded. 'Any time.'

'Have a good day at uni,' said Baz.

Daisy waved and set off. When she opened the café door to leave, an Asian man ducked through the door and called out a cheerful, 'Wagwan, ladies?'

Baz battled two forces inside her: one compelling her to be friendly and the other pressuring her to side with her friends in their dislike of this man. She gave as bland a smile as she could manage. 'Morning, Clive.'

Madge sucked air through her teeth. 'Clive.'

Peggy's lip curled. 'Say what you want, Clive.'

Clive clutched his hand to his chest. 'What? Can't I just come to say hello?'

'You could.' Peggy's voice was cold. 'But you don't — ergo, you didn't.'

'Yes, well. Be that as it may...' Clive's eyes slid around the room, checking to see who else might be within earshot. 'I just heard a juicy bit of gossip and I thought you might find it interesting.'

Peggy's fingers tapped away on her keyboard. Without looking up, she said, 'Is this about the so-called Goldsmiths Groper?'

Clive shook his head. 'No, it's about...' The man's shoulders sagged. 'That handsome cop... You heard already.'

'Of course we did. Not a thing goes on in Deptford or New Cross that we don't know about.' Madge made an impatient shooing gesture.

Clive pulled a disappointed face. 'Well, fine then. I suppose I'll just get my coffee and go.'

'You do that,' said Carole, her needles still clicking away.

Peggy carried on tapping up a storm on her keyboard as Clive headed back through to the other room. Both Carole and Madge's needles were clacking away as they worked on their respective knitting projects. Even Cookie was busy chewing on his crocheted human heart.

Baz pulled her embroidery from her bag and got to work.

————

Thank you for reading my little book. I hope you enjoyed it.

If you're not already on my email list, you can join it now and get a free story.

Click the image to download Friends in Need for free

the end (for now)

Thank you for reading *A Bit of Murder Between Friends*, the first novel in the *Vigilauntie Justice series*.

My success or failure as an indie author depends largely on word-of-mouth recommendations. If you enjoyed this book, please consider leaving a review. And honestly, if you despised this book with the very fibre of your soul ... **please leave a review**.

Baz, Peggy, Carole, and Madge will almost certainly continue their mission to keep south-east London safe.

acknowledgements

I've spent the last few years immersed in a science-fictional universe. All my life, I've loved sci-fi. But I also love crime fiction: mysteries, thrillers, cosies, whatever.

Near the end of 2022, I was in a crime-y sort of mood, reading-wise. I quite often read two books at a time and, this time, I was reading Richard Osman's *The Thursday Murder Club* and Helene Tursten's *An Elderly Lady Is Up to No Good*. The combination of the two set my brain off in a 'what if' spiral.

As a sci-fi author, I really don't have enough books out there to go switching genres and pen names. But, as a neurodivergent human, if I want to write anything at all, I have to go where my muse leads.

The muse is a harsh mistress.

Anyways.

Over the next few days, Peggy, Carole, Madge, and Baz bubbled to the surface of my brain.

So, even though they'll never read this, I owe a big thank you to Richard Osman and Helene Tursten. And to Michael Aitkens, the writer of the 1990s BBC sitcom *Waiting for God* – another person who'll never read my thanks. Still.

Moving on to the people who may actually read these words...

Thanks especially to both Charlie Stross and Vanessa Snipe for both (independently, I might add) suggesting the same method of <ahem> dealing with the Goldsmiths Groper.

As always, the WiFi Sci-Fi writers' group has been the most

amazing gift. They continually teach, push, and cheerlead me to be a better writer. And they provided much needed feedback on the first chapter of this story.

I want to thank my beta readers: Dave Walsh, Stephanie Francis, and Julie Golden. They all got stuck right into the guts of my ridiculous tale and helped provide a buff and polish.

Michelle and Hannah, my editors, dug into the meat of this vegetarian story to make it the best version of itself it could be. Any mistakes you find now are entirely my own fault.

And to all the people on social media who've responded to my endless posts about this series with some variation of 'Little old ladies who murder people? Sign me up!' This one's for you – freaks and weirdos, the lot of you.

Finally, my legally contracted lifemate, Dave, has been putting up with more than any human being should have to. If you've ever met me in real life, you'll understand what a big deal that is. Seriously ... I'm *a lot*. Dave has listened to me talk about my imaginary friends every single day for six years. Dave's the best person.

about the author

ELLIOTT HAY (any pronouns) dreams of a world where nice little old ladies don't have to <ahem> take matters into their own hands.

They also write sci-fi under the name Si Clarke.

BV - #0139 - 240723 - C0 - 198/129/12 - PB - 9781739768133 - Matt Lamination